But then the crowd parted and the man stepped into full view.

And Mila froze.

She wondered for a moment if she'd simply died where she stood—or possibly it was only that she wished she had.

He was looking right at her.

With that trademark near smirk in the corner of his appallingly sensual mouth.

Because he was the only person in the entire world who knew the truth that Mila preferred to believe only she knew. That Queen Emilia of Las Sosegadas was not the least bit perfect.

He was Caius Candriano.

Mila's one and only mistake.

And he was also, though no one knew this but the two of them nor ever would as long as she drew breath, still—legally—her husband.

USA TODAY bestselling, RITA® Award—nominated and critically acclaimed author **Caitlin Crews** has written more than one hundred and thirty books and counting. She has a master's and PhD in English literature, thinks everyone should read more category romance and is always available to discuss her beloved alpha heroes—just ask. She lives in the Pacific Northwest with her comic book—artist husband, is always planning her next trip and will never, ever read all the books in her to-be-read pile. Thank goodness.

Books by Caitlin Crews

Harlequin Presents

A Secret Heir to Secure His Throne
What Her Sicilian Husband Desires
A Billion-Dollar Heir for Christmas
Wedding Night in the King's Bed
Her Venetian Secret

The Outrageous Accardi Brothers

The Christmas He Claimed the Secretary
The Accidental Accardi Heir

Innocent Stolen Brides

The Desert King's Kidnapped Virgin
The Spaniard's Last-Minute Wife

The Teras Wedding Challenge

A Tycoon Too Wild to Wed

The Diamond Club

Pregnant Princess Bride

Visit the Author Profile page
at Harlequin.com for more titles.

FORBIDDEN ROYAL VOWS

CAITLIN CREWS

PRESENTS

ISBN-13: 978-1-335-93908-1

Forbidden Royal Vows

For questions and comments about the quality of this book, please contact us at CustomerService@Harlequin.com.

TM and ® are trademarks of Harlequin Enterprises ULC.

 Harlequin Enterprises ULC
22 Adelaide St. West, 41st Floor
Toronto, Ontario M5H 4E3, Canada
www.Harlequin.com

Printed in Lithuania

Recycling programs for this product may not exist in your area.

MIX
Paper | Supporting responsible forestry
FSC® C021394

FORBIDDEN ROYAL VOWS

This one is for Nicole, who was halfway through Carliz's book when she said she couldn't wait to read Mila's...the one that hadn't occurred to me I should write until then!

CHAPTER ONE

QUEEN EMILIA OF LAS SOSEGADAS was perfect.

She made sure of it.

Las Sosegadas was a tiny country between France and Spain, all mountains and sparkling alpine lakes. Her family had ruled it for centuries, mostly in peace. And her people were consistently at the top of all the polls that measured the happiest citizens in the European Union.

And unlike some other kingdoms, support of *her* monarchy was always robust.

Because, she knew, she was perfect.

Perfection wasn't simply her job. It was her calling. Her duty.

She spent hours every day discussing exactly how the Queen could appear to her best advantage in all things, not because she had an ego, because she didn't. What she had was a crown and what she owed her subjects was to keep it untarnished.

In private, she could be a person. Even a woman.

In private, she still thought of herself as Mila, the nickname only her sister still called her. Even her mother called her *Your Majesty* now, likely to remind herself as much as anyone else that it was her daughter on the throne now instead of her late husband.

There were a lot of things Mila liked about being *just Mila*, but that was always a temporary state, mostly when she was asleep.

The moment she left her rooms and let anyone lay eyes on her, she was the paragon of a modern queen she always was. In public, Mila was only and ever *the Queen*.

She had promised herself to her country and that was that.

A life of service suited her perfectly, she always said, and she meant it.

Tonight her service to her country had involved the sort of dress fitting that had taken most of the afternoon. It was always necessary to make sure that she looked the part, of course. She had an entire wardrobe team dedicated to the task and they were good at what they did.

What Mila had to do in turn was always and ever appear *relatable*. But not *too* relatable. Subjects wanted to love their Queen, but they certainly didn't want to know her *too* well. A simple flip through the headlines of any European kingdom on any given day told her as much.

Mila had to strike a balance between seeming *almost* approachable while never actually letting anyone near enough to get any fingerprints on the symbol she'd become in her short reign.

Figurative fingerprints, that was. Or the Royal Guards would get involved.

Tonight's event was a banquet to honor service to the crown, an annual gala that also raised money for various charities. It was the usual collection of aristocrats, Mila saw at a glance as she arrived, her foot hitting the exact stone that she had promised it would hit at the exact time it had been announced she would.

Because it was always important to be a *dependable* icon, no matter what else she was.

Sometimes Mila thought it was all she was.

If so, she thought now, *there are far worse things I could be.*

And she did not list off what those things were, as she sometimes did. She already knew that did not lead to perfection. It went the other way, rather precipitously.

She swept through her usual protocols for these things. The selected greetings after her entrance. The few, carefully chosen comments to make it clear that she knew the people she was speaking to. Even a smile now and again.

Mila had always been good at these things. She'd always known how to make these little connections, over so quickly, feel bigger than the sum of their parts. Because she had not been thrown into the royal life in a turbulent fashion. She'd had the gift and curse of knowing that her father was not only going to have to die *someday* for her to succeed him, but that the doctors had given him a date by which they expected that to occur.

There were very few good things about that, but one of them—maybe the only one—was that he had taken the time to prepare her appropriately for what was to come. And not in the abstract, as she'd been taught as a child.

She had no regrets, she told herself.

What was there to regret? She was the Queen.

"You are looking splendid, Your Majesty," said her mother from her side as they left the receiving line and processed through the party, headed for the Queen's usual spot on a dais up near the throne. Mila inclined her head, lest anyone think she was engaging in something as base as small talk or gossip while the trumpets were playing.

Was it ostentatious to have balls take place in front of the throne of the kingdom? Certainly. On the other hand, she had been told many times that most people appreciated the touch of glamour.

Besides, it was expected.

No point going all the way to a palace and not experiencing anything palatial, now, is there? her sister, Carliz, would have said if she was there.

Mila let her lips curve with great serenity as she passed the line of bowing subjects. But inside, she felt that surprising pang again.

She didn't know why it had not occurred to her that she would miss her sister.

When Carliz had gone off to university, the first one in the family to leave the kingdom to do so, she had been younger and consumed with learning her duties as Crown Princess. It wasn't that she hadn't missed her then, because she had.

But it was different this time.

She had gotten used to having Carliz here, was the thing. She had gotten used to her sister slipping into her room at night, when Her Majesty was left at the door and Mila could simply be Mila again. They had spent most of a summer that way and Mila had gotten used to it. She had come to rely on it, even. That was all.

It wasn't that she would change a thing. She was too happy for Carliz, who had gone from being one of the world's greatest sparkling It girls to about the happiest wife and mother Mila had ever seen.

But she could be happy for Carliz and sad for herself, it turned out.

I contain multitudes, she thought as she moved, practicing the dignified inclination of her head which she could often use in place of actual speech, or even a smile.

This was one of the great many ways she got people to forget how very young she was.

Only twenty-seven, though that was rarely mentioned in the way it had been at first, when her father had died and the whole of Europe had acted as if they didn't know what an *heir apparent* was.

Now when they said *"only twenty-seven"* it was in tones of awe, as if no one could quite credit that she was still something less than the formidable dowager of indeterminate years she would be one day. The one she had gotten so good at pretending she already was.

If everything went according to plan, she would simply grow grayer but otherwise remain exactly the same.

The Queen, nothing more and nothing less.

As ageless as the currency she graced.

Her mother was murmuring to her as they walked, the usual comments about this noblewoman's dress or that aristocrat's wandering eye, because nobody minded if the Queen Mother offered commentary. And the dancing had begun, so there was no shortage of things to look at.

"And, of course, we are treated to the next regrettable stop along Lady Paula's road to ruin," her mother was tutting at her side. "I often look at her and think, there but for the grace of God above did your poor sister go."

Mila was entirely too well-trained to react broadly enough that anyone could see it. All she did was slide a look her mother's way. Nothing more. She did not even have to raise an eyebrow.

Still, the Queen Mother blew out a breath, aware that she had stumbled into one of the places she should know better than to go.

As Mila had made her feelings on this clear. As the Queen.

"My sister," Mila said softly, smiling magnificently at a set of honorees as she passed them, dipped down low into their curtseys, "would never dream of embarrassing me. And she never did. Lady Paula, who I think you know I quite like, has a different goal entirely in mind."

She did not go so far as to say, *I support her.*

But she was defending her, so that should have been obvious.

"You may judge me if you like," her mother replied in that particularly aggrieved tone she was so good at pulling out at moments like this, as if Mila had thrown her in the dungeons. If the palace had actually *had* dungeons, which it did not, she might have considered it— for the express purpose of watching expression on her mother's face. But that was childish. And the Queen could never be childish. Even when she'd been a child, it had been discouraged. "But I cannot for the life of me understand what it is Lady Paula is so upset about. Many women of her station are called upon to make life choices that honor their family legacy, not their own wild impulses."

It was well known that Lady Paula's father wished to marry her off to a man of his choosing. Lady Paula had made certain that no one in the whole of the kingdom could think for one moment that this was something she approved. Or would ever approve. She had gone to great lengths to make sure that her disapproval was recorded in the starkest possible terms in every tabloid that could be found.

With as many inappropriate men she could find, to her father's fury.

"Maybe it's time that we allowed women of whatever station to choose their own destinies," Mila said.

Reasonably enough, to her mind.

The look her mother shot her was sharp. Too sharp for a public setting, Mila would have thought. "I hope you do not intend to follow Lady Paula's example. Your Majesty."

That was a shot and they both knew it.

Mila smiled as they came to a stop before the throne, because it was considered gaudy and inappropriate for her to guffaw. Or so she had been told, never having given in to the urge in public before.

"I know my duty, Mother," she said softly. "I daresay I know it better than most."

"Of course you do, my dear," her mother replied, though they both knew that if it were up to her, the Queen Mother would be planning the sovereign's wedding here and now.

And when she turned away to talk brightly to the people who came up on the other side, as if she hadn't been squabbling with the Queen herself, Mila took a moment to gaze out at the whirling mass of dancers before her, looking for that telltale flash that was always Lady Paula's orange-red hair.

When they'd been girls, Paula had won her friendship forever by wrinkling up her nose and laughing too loudly at a party where they were all attempting to out-ladylike each other, and then announcing quite boldly that as her hair was already problematic, she saw no particular reason not to make sure her behavior matched it.

Mila heard Paula's laugh before she saw her. She was already smiling as she realized her friend had drawn near the way she usually did, moving along the sides of the ball that was in full swing across the floor of the great room. She turned her head, expecting to see what she normally did when Paula attended one of these parties.

Her friend always dressed *almost* inappropriately, but not quite, because it drove her staid and quiet family mad. And she took pride in always presenting herself in the company of some or other wildly inappropriate date, and then presenting said date to her friend—the Queen.

Usually Mila made it worse, according to her mother, by indulging Paula in this. Meaning she only smiled at her friend's behavior when, as queen, she could also have indicated her displeasure.

That would not have stopped Paula, but it would have meant she had one less friend, and Mila had never seen the point.

She had so few as it was.

"Don't start," she warned her mother beneath her breath as Paula drew close.

Her mother sniffed in reply.

But then the crowd parted way and the man Paula was leading toward the throne stepped into full view.

And Mila froze.

She wondered for a moment if she'd simply died where she stood— or possibly it was only that she wished she had.

Because tonight it wasn't just any old inappropriate man on Paula's arm. This or that baronet from some country Mila hardly knew.

Tonight, it was the most inappropriate man Mila had ever met.

And he was looking right at her.

With that trademark near-smirk in the corner of his appallingly sensual mouth.

Because he was the only person in the entire world who knew the truth that Mila preferred to believe only she knew. That Queen Emilia of Las Sosegadas was not the least bit perfect.

He was, in fact, the only one who knew that she was capable of an epic, life-altering, unforgivable error of judgment.

Not just *capable* of it.

He was one of the last great European playboys in the old style, a recent article in a non-tabloid magazine had claimed quite seriously. And had backed it up.

He was famous for his long string of astonishingly beautiful, powerful, and famous lovers, his mesmerizing charm that Hollywood actors tried and failed to replicate onscreen, his deeply mutable moral code that some found charming, and the great fortunes he'd inherited from all branches of his enormously complicated family tree.

A tree, the article had claimed, that has its roots in every grand old family in Europe.

Worse than all that, he was impossibly, disastrously attractive.

A description of him would involve dark hair, dark eyes, and those cheekbones, but it would fail entirely to capture the way he moved through a room like the world was nothing but a crock of creamery butter waiting for the edge of his knife.

And she knew that he always, always, had that knife.

He was always perfectly dressed for every occasion, yet managed to provoke all the same. It was that swagger. It was that hint of a smirk. It was that lazy wit in his gaze, and his inability to show even the faintest bit of humility to stations higher than his own.

It was the fact that he could be so incisive. That he was so intelligent when there should have been nothing but air and smugness between his temples.

It was the formidable way he could gaze at a person and make them forget who they were without even seeming to try—

Mila had to remind herself to maintain her composure. She had to *order herself* not to lose her cool, right here in the middle of a gala.

Something she had not had to do since she was a child of eight who had accidentally indulged in too much sugar one Christmas.

But he was a whole lot worse than too many sweets at a holiday party.

He was a *catastrophe*.

He was Caius Candriano.

Mila's one and only mistake.

And he was also, though no one knew this but the two of them nor ever would as long as she drew breath, still—legally—her husband.

CHAPTER TWO

CAIUS CANDRIANO HAD waited for this day for a long, long time.

Five years, to be exact.

Five whole years, and there was some part of him that expected to find her...different, perhaps. Changed entirely by what she'd gone through and who she'd become these last few years—perhaps because that, at least, would be some kind of explanation.

However little he wished to accept that explanation, at least it would exist.

After all, she was a queen now. *The Queen.* Not merely the Princess he had met with the whole of her weighty future yet before her. Not that young woman with too much maturity and luminous eyes, and a deathly ill father who had ordered her to in that sense that she was only marking time before her whole world changed.

But Mila looked entirely unchanged.

Maybe that was not entirely true, he thought as he swept a gaze over the whole of her magnificence, when the woman he'd known had been dressed as casually as he had been on that long-ago climb up a remote stretch of California coast where there had been no one at all but the two of them. Though the drama of the gown she wore would have been epic even if he wasn't comparing her to his memories.

Caius should not have been surprised. He was fully aware that designers from all over the fashionable world clamored for the opportunity to dress the young, beloved Queen of Las Sosegadas.

It was his own curse that he knew too well that, left to her own devices, she preferred simpler, less theatrical fare.

Not that anyone could have guessed that by looking at her.

She *gleamed* with her own consequence. The palace arranged around her, complete with the throne placed *just so* behind her, only made her glory more apparent. He might miss the days he'd known her out of time and place, but there was no denying that gown suited *this* version of Mila. Her team had clearly chosen it to make her seem to glow as if by virtue of her own sovereign power.

The Queen had been the only thing anyone had looked at when she appeared. The Queen had been gazed at in varying degrees of awe and adoration from all corners as she'd made her way across the floor of the long ballroom, the traditional signal that the festivities were to begin.

The gown helped, though Caius found himself simmering with what he decided could only be the same old pent-up *fury* that really, she could have sloped across the ballroom floor in jeans and trainers and had much the same effect.

He focused on the gown, because that was smarter than looking straight at her when he could not be entirely sure that he had his face in proper order. When he had been born the chameleon he was today, a necessity in his family, chock full of narcissists and pathological liars—and that was just the people he was related to that he liked.

Caius took in the sophistication and elegance of the damned dress. He focused on the full skirt and fitted bodice that should have made the dress too undignified for a queen, but was saved by its deep, dark shade of purple. It suited her. Something about the conversation between the dress's serious color and merrier shape made Mila's regrettably perfect beauty all the brighter.

He wished it did not still light him up from within, damn her.

Though that was not the point of this.

This, he reminded himself, was about *a reckoning*, nothing more.

Because Queen Emilia was suitably untouchable and all the more breathtaking for it. But Mila was the kind of woman a man looked at once and found himself intoxicated evermore. She was like a flickering flame. Once a man singed himself on the edge of that fire, he could never come back.

He had never come back. And she had never looked back.

So Caius had come to her little palace in the mountains instead.

She wore a tiara tonight, in case the throne behind her did not give away her status. The bejeweled concoction sat on her smooth, glossy dark hair that looked like ink tamed into a sophisticated twist and dared any man brave enough to reach out and try to touch her.

Though he did not. And not because he was lacking in bravery. On the contrary, he had only recently taken a step back from his more high-octane activities, all of them death-defying, and only because he had done them all.

Even adrenaline got boring if you had too much of it.

But he had chosen this battle specifically, and there was no point getting ahead of himself now when he'd gone to all the trouble to ingratiate himself with half the aristocracy in this tiny country. Something that had involved him deigning to notice them, since he was, being himself, far more famous and sought after than a host of interchangeable blue bloods.

That was not arrogance on his part. It was a simple truth.

He had often been called the most beloved guest in modern Europe. That was partly because he was a great delight, if he said so himself. But it was also because his attendance at any given party made it *the* party.

That, too, was simply a fact.

Really, the monarchy of Las Sosegadas should *thank him* for deigning to attend at all.

Caius lifted his gaze to hers at last, taking no small amount of pleasure in how stunned Mila looked. There was no trace of anything he would call *thankful* on that gaze of hers, a perfect oval saved from any insipid sameness by that strong, Roman nose that made her something else than simply *pretty*. That and her mouth, a wide, sensual feast that she mostly kept pressed into a dutiful line.

Though not now, he was pleased to see.

And there was something in the gray depths of her gaze, rimmed in a darker steel, that he recognized. It shot through him like more of that inescapable flame, though he doubted she would appreciate it if he reminded her where and when he'd seen a look like that before.

That made him want to tell her even more.

Because none of this was about what she appreciated.

If she had wanted him to consider such things, she would have handled the past five years much, much differently.

On the other hand, he did have a plan. Such as it was.

So he only held her gaze, which was not exactly good etiquette. Not so directly. Not for so long. But more tellingly, she continued to stare back.

And Caius had watched enough videos of Queen Emilia's much-swooned-over perfect manners to know that this was unusual.

As it damn well should be, he thought then.

Next to the Queen, her mother, once Queen Alondra and now the Queen Mother, clearly noted that something was amiss. She drew herself up with a sideways glance at her daughter for only the briefest, nearly imperceptible instant before stepping forward and claiming Lady Paula's attention.

"I trust your parents are well?" the older woman asked, with a bite behind her words that even he could hear. Clearly Paula could as well, because she let out that high-spirited laugh of hers again, infectious enough to make Caius almost wish that he had it in him to move on.

But he could not seem to break his stare. He could not look away from Mila.

And as he watched, he saw the Mila he had known five years ago first bloom in her expression, then disappear again.

Until *the Queen* took her place.

She made the transition very clear and unmistakable. It was something about her posture. Something about the tilt of her head, or perhaps the elongation of her neck. One perfect dark brow rose, just slightly.

Yet still elegantly.

"I forget myself, Your Majesty," Caius said, and he could see that his voice affected her. He saw the faint hint of color on her cheeks. That glimmer in her gray gaze.

He still got to her. That was good.

Caius had not exactly planned what he might do if she looked at him as if he was a stranger. He had not allowed it as a possibility.

Instead of interrogating himself on that topic he executed a bow so deep and so perfect that it bordered on parody. That was the point. She had once accused him of using his grasp of excruciatingly proper and gloriously correct manners as a weapon. So efficiently and so ruthlessly that he was already bludgeoning the haughty and the arrogant before they even realized there was a weapon in the room.

Guilty as charged, he had said.

And it felt like a bit of poetic justice that he was now using those weapons on her.

He could see that she remembered that same conversation when he rose and met her gaze again. He could see the knowledge there, the memory. He could almost smell the sea air and feel the crackle of the fire they'd built, the flame a wild heat against his face.

He was not the only one recalling what had come after.

"Your Majesty," said Alondra from the side, warningly, though Caius did not bother to look away from Mila, "Lady Paula has kindly come to present the Honorable Caius Candriano, late of Italy."

Caius looked at the Queen Mother then, and bowed again more shallowly. "I am afraid I have not been to Italy in some while, ma'am. Nor can I claim to be anything like honorable."

He lifted his head and grinned at Mila's poor mother, who was very clearly both unamused by him...and yet amused despite herself.

That was the Caius effect.

"Your mother does not approve of me," Paula was saying to Mila with more of that laughter, because she was a free-spirited thing and had no qualms about showing it, a rarity in these circles. She looked back at the Queen Mother. "You may wish to remove yourself from this conversation. I do not censor myself in front of my queen."

"Or anywhere else," said the acerbic older woman, but she did move away at that—with shoulders set to angles of pure umbrage.

Paula gave the impression of moving in close to the Queen, though she did not actually scale the dais or step up, or even encroach particularly on Mila as she stood there in all her state. Close enough to the great throne that not sitting on it seemed like more of a power move than sprawling there might have.

He had no doubt at all that it was deliberate, and more, that it was her doing.

"You've heard of Caius, of course," Paula was saying happily, and did not seem to see the nearly pained look on Mila's face. "My grandmother had a *conniption fit* when I announced that I would be attending with him. A proper fit of the vapors. Though I maintain that if she knows of his exploits, that must mean that she has the very lowbrow taste she *claims* to abhor."

Mila made a low sort of noise that Caius supposed could be taken for assent. Paula leaned a bit closer and continued chattering on about her own reputation, and making shocking asides about Caius's—shocking, that was, only because he had been *much worse* in the time period she was referencing, and had worked hard at being that notorious.

It was only when Mila still kept standing there in the same way, looking dumbstruck at Caius—though he supposed it was possible no one else understood that he was the cause of it—that Paula subsided.

"You seem a bit out of it tonight," she said in a different tone. One that indicated, immediately, that the woman who had been nothing but laughter and fun thus far was, truly, the friend to Mila it was rumored she was. "Are you all right? Is it Carliz?"

Mila looked away from him at last, and he hated that.

But then she smiled, and the smile made him forget where he was. "Carliz is fine. More than fine. Carliz is *great*."

Caius remembered himself, despite that unexpected shine and the way it was as if all the light in the room had clung to her like that. He did not shake it off, not physically, but he stood there, calculating. Taking stock of the fact that Mila clearly favored Paula, as some had said and others had debated. She *liked* Paula.

And he wasn't sure he liked the part of him that was glad of that. He remembered too well the confessions she'd made to him on that long trek they'd taken together. How little she could trust that anyone truly liked *her*. That the specter of the queen she would become was always there between them.

"She seems deliriously happy," Paula was saying. "Truly happy, not simply a bit of Carliz sparkle."

The two of them spoke for a few moments longer, and he watched her eyes light up the way they always had at the mention of her sister.

But then it was time for the best part of this entire scene he had gone to such trouble to engineer.

No one got to stand and talk to a queen for long. There were always interfering ministers about. There were always haughty people who thought it was their *right* to demand a moment with her. There were long lines of those who only wished to curtsey before her and see if they could get a small smile, a kind word. Like she was an art installation.

It was not a surprise when Alondra reappeared, tugging on her left earlobe in what seemed like a casual gesture. But Caius knew it was a sign to her daughter that it was time to move on.

"We must catch up properly," Mila said. "Have you seen all of Carliz's baby pictures?"

Paula sighed. "She keeps promising to send them."

"Something will have to be done." But as Mila said that, she straightened, and Caius watched with interest as she became *the Queen* once again. Not chilly, but remote.

Paula understood at once. She reached for Caius's arm and stepped back, then curtsied yet again. Beside her, Caius bowed, a gesture replete with all the mockery he could manage.

And then he had the very great pleasure of walking away from Her Majesty, Queen Emilia of Las Sosegadas, and not looking back.

He didn't have to look back.

Caius could feel her eyes on him no matter where he went in the ballroom. When he danced with Paula, or the much older ladies who he always liked to favor with his attention because they saw right through him and basked in him anyway. Even when he loitered about near the bar, making pointless conversation with interchangeable nobles.

He made certain to spend the night paying her not the slightest iota of attention.

But just as he, and everyone else, knew exactly where Queen Emilia was at all times, he knew full well that she was returning the favor where he was concerned.

Caius could feel it like her hands on him.

When the banquet was over and all the speeches had been made, and more dancing had taken place until well past midnight, he offered his date his arm as they walked out of the palace with the rest of the guests.

And he felt pure triumph kick in him when an aide stepped smartly to Paula's side. "Lady Paula, if you'd be so kind, the staff have assembled a selection of Princess Carliz's private photos for your perusal at the behest of the Queen. If you have a moment."

"For Carliz, I have all the moments," Paula proclaimed grandly. She was slightly tipsy and even more boisterous than before, and she waved Caius off as she followed the aide away. "Don't get yourself in any trouble," she called back over her shoulder.

Then laughed as she disappeared out of sight.

But even if Caius had been intending to get himself into trouble, he could not. Because another aide appeared at his side, then. This aide only bowed and indicated that Caius should follow him. Then, wordlessly, led him away.

It did not occur to Caius to resist.

He thrust his hands into his pockets, and sloped along after his guide. And he was not the least bit surprised to find himself taken away from the public areas of the palace and into a quieter, lusher wing.

The aide led him down the long, intricately decorated hall and stopped abruptly at a particular door. He knocked three times, then waited for a signal only he seemed to hear.

But hear it he did, for he clicked his heels, bowed his head, and pulled open the door to let Caius inside.

He found himself in a small salon that did not look as if it saw great deal of traffic. And Caius could admit that he was surprised to find himself alone—

But no. Not quite.

Across the room, there were doors that led outside. He went over, looked out, and there she was.

She was standing out on a balcony, her back to him and her gaze focused on her kingdom's capital, arranged neatly below the palace and marching in tidy lines around the first of the many alpine lakes that were considered the beating heart of this country.

Or so he had read.

Extensively.

He stayed where he was, on his side of the glass, because everything in him was a drumbeat now. Blood too hot in his veins. Pulse pounding like he'd jumped from a plane. She was leaning forward, her elbows propped on the stone railing, and if he was a painter his hands would have itched to capture this moment. The Queen in a moment of reflection. The Queen's quiet contemplation of the weight of her crown.

Though he knew what she was actually considering just now was the weight of him.

His body hard over hers. His mouth to hers. His—

Caius made himself pause. He made himself *breathe*.

And then he stepped out onto the balcony himself. And thrust his untrustworthy hands in his pockets as he moved to stand beside her.

She did not look at him. He did not look at her.

But for a long moment, there was only this. The two of them, breathing in the same air after so long.

"I can only assume that this is some kind of a threat, Caius," she said, eventually. Softly, even.

She was still looking away from him. When he glanced at her, he could see the line of her face, the nose that defined her face and made her so stunning, the shape of her lips. But he could not read the expression in her gaze, or even if there was one.

"I'm not a man who needs to issue threats, *Your Majesty*." He even laughed a little. "I would have thought that you would know this already."

"It's been five years. I assumed that you'd slithered off, never to be seen again. To be clear, I hoped you had."

She turned then, straightening from the rail and folding her arms over her chest, which he understood in an instant was as close as he would get to an outward expression of her emotional state. *The Queen*, obviously, did not cross her arms.

Yet he had known her as a woman first. He could see the things she hid. The sheen in her gaze that spoke of her feelings. The barest, faintest hint of a tremble in her lush lower lip.

This was likely to be all the temper she was willing to show him.

He'd take it. Because he could see the truth of it.

"Careful," he murmured. "That is no way to speak to your husband."

"What is it you want?" And her voice was so cool. Her gaze was frosted over. But he was close enough, outside on this clear fall night with the canopy of stars above, to see the pulse in her throat that gave her away even further.

"What is it you think I want?"

They stared at each other, and it was as if the earth and the sky switched places. As if he was standing half in each, not sure if there was solid ground above his head or stars at his feet.

"As you might imagine, the pressure to marry is intense," she told him in that grave, measured manner that he had studied, these last few years. He'd seen it in so many news programs. In every clip of her speaking that he could locate online. "At a certain point, my protestations that I wish to stand on my own two feet will have to give way to the best interests of the kingdom. Those being, of course, that I will be required to produce my own heir."

"Mila," he murmured, and it was possible he moved a bit closer, too, "that sounds a great deal like your problem, not mine."

Her gaze was dark and gray. "I understand that vows mean nothing to you. But I'm afraid I take mine rather seriously."

"Nothing has changed since the last time we had this delightful chat," he said in the same quiet way that tore at him, so he suspected it shredded her, too. "I invite you to divorce me, as I have done from the start."

"You know that I can't."

"Then I can only repeat what I told you five years ago. If you do not wish to divorce—"

"Of course I want to divorce." And whatever it was that flashed in her gaze, that slap of emotion, he could feel it in him, too. Low. Deep. Much too dangerous, the way it always had been between them. "But you refuse to sign the documents that I would need for that to happen."

"I've already kept our marriage confidential," he said with a shrug that, very likely, did not match the edge in his voice. "I do not see why you cannot simply trust me to keep our divorce equally private."

"I have never understood why you insist on playing these power games." But there was no heat behind the words. If anything, she sounded weary, and that felt like a weapon of her own, sunk deep. "What do you hope to gain? At the end of the day I will always be, until the day of my death, the Queen of the Sosegadas. And you—"

"Yes, me," he said when she paused. "There's nothing about me that is not indiscreet, is that not so?" He made himself a portrait of sheer indolence, standing there so languidly, and perhaps it was for the sky above. Perhaps it was for her. Perhaps it was entirely self-referential—or perhaps it was that or put his hands on her the way he deeply, darkly wanted to. "My own parents appear to be engaged in a competition to see who can collect the most spouses in one lifetime. Mine is less a family tree, and more…a collection of misbegotten sticks that someone gripped in a careless hand, then threw up into the sky, not caring at all where they might land. This must be so distressing for you."

"Again." And this time, her voice was resignation and steel at once. "What is it you *want*?"

"Perhaps I think it is time you finally recognize me," he said. And then he tilted his chin down so he could look at her and not the stars. So he could bask a little in that look of sheer horror on her face. "Oh, dear. Does that not fit into your plans? What *would* the good people of your kingdom think if they knew you had married so disastrously? If they had any idea you were swept away like a foolish girl, enslaved entirely by your body's demands? What will they think of their spotless queen then?"

"They would assume what I have assumed ever since," she said in that same calm voice, but he could see her eyes. He could see the way they'd gone a little hectic. "You are a master seducer, as you have proven repeatedly. I succumbed, as many do regularly, according to your rather overactive tabloid profile. Life is filled with regrets. The end."

"I can see that you put thought into that one," Caius said, sounding almost congratulatory. "No doubt you practiced it in the royal mirror. But the tragedy remains the same, does it not, my queen? In order to brand me a base seducer, you must cast yourself as the seduced. And who will consider you an icon above all others then? You will be but one more pathetic creature, ensnared like so many women are by men so unsavory that any association with them leaves a mark."

Mila only raised a cool brow. "How lovely that at least one person on this planet appreciates my dilemma."

He laughed at that, a low sound that the stars stole away. But he saw the color rise in her face, and then everything was fire.

"Poor little Majesty," he murmured. "It appears that you remain hoist securely on your own petard."

Her cheeks were aflame but her voice was still cool. "We will have to find a solution, Caius. You must know that."

"I require no solutions. I am perfectly content."

"Then why are you here?"

Caius laughed again. "When have I ever given you the impression that I'm the sort of person who would not enjoy a moment like this?" Her face looked hotter, and he could feel his own temperature rising. He told himself it was temper. Well-deserved temper. "You can't control this, Mila. You can't control me."

"I have no wish to control you. The world is yours, Caius. Go be as uncontrolled as you like, with my blessing. Only let me end this marriage first."

But he was on a roll. And he didn't believe in her blessings anyway. "This palace is yours. All of these people, yours. Yet you and I know that where it matters, Mila, you have been and always will be mine."

Again, he saw the way her gaze flared with temper,

though there was otherwise little sign of it on her face. Maybe her jaw was more firm, but that was all. "This isn't a game, Caius."

"But to me, everything is." He leaned in then, so close but he did not reach for her. And the sharp pleasure of denying himself almost gave way to the bright flame of indulgence. *Almost.* "Have you forgotten when you said that to me? Because I have not, Mila. I have not forgotten one word."

"I was not trying to insult you. I was trying to explain."

And years had passed. He believed her. She had, truly, simply been explaining her position to him, but in a way, that made it all the more insulting. Had she been *trying* to insult him, he would have been able to dismiss the things she'd said. Standing there so earnestly before him after the time they'd shared.

But she had been trying to be kind. He remembered that part too well. That had made it worse.

That had made it unforgivable.

"You have had the opportunity to change," she said now, and there was a different sort of tension in the way she held herself, then. "It is impossible to avoid your exploits, and believe me, I have tried. So instead, I watched them. I watched you. I waited to see if even the slightest, faintest hint that anything I'd said to you had landed. If you'd thought for even one moment about my position, or what I need—"

"There was a time when I thought of nothing else."

And it was not perhaps the greatest strategy to say something like that so boldly, with so little finesse.

Then again, maybe it was the best strategy, because he heard her breath hitch. He watched, transfixed, as she lifted one hand and held it to her neck as if attempting to conceal the way her pulse pounded.

But he could see the way her fingers shook.

It should have made him feel small, the way that echoed in him like a new heat. Like a blessing all its own.

Luckily Caius was not that kind of man.

There was nothing small about him.

"You can't want money," she said after a moment, insulting him anew. "Can you?"

"Perhaps you have forgotten that I have too many fortunes to name," he said, and this time, he forgot to keep the danger from his voice. Because she was even more maddening up close than she had been from afar all these years. He had not expected that. "Perhaps you have forgotten everything."

"I have forgotten nothing," she shot back.

"All the same," he said, turning toward her at last and feeling that same electricity flood him the way it had since the moment they'd clapped eyes on each other, all those years ago and now again, too, "I think a small reminder is in order. To remind us who we are, *Your Majesty*."

And he did not wait for her raised brow, her queenly armor.

He did not wait for her response at all.

Caius simply hooked a palm around the nape of her neck, aware that she still fit him perfectly.

Then he pulled her to him and kissed her the way he'd wanted to for years.

CHAPTER THREE

MILA TASTED HIM again and died.

Or maybe it was that she came back to life.

It was that intense, that glorious, the way it always had been. The way she had known it would be from the start. The way he had showed her it could be between them.

And tonight his kiss sent her spiraling back through time.

Straight back into all the things she'd forgotten—or tried her very best to forget, with failures she only admitted to in the very dark of night. Then tried to deny come morning.

He took her mouth the way he always had, as if he knew her body and its needs better than she ever could. It was deep, familiar shock of pure desire, as expansive and overwhelming as all of that California sunshine mixed in with days of intense fog that they'd once walked through together.

It was everything she missed and pretended she didn't. Because she couldn't.

And it was also a deep and enduring grief, washing over her, through her, making the intensity of the kiss seem to roll through her so hard and wild she was surprised, on some level, that it didn't knock her off the balcony.

Mila forgot all these years of duty, just the way she had before. She forgot the promises she'd made, the vows she had spoken with such deep solemnity in front of the country and the world.

She forgot everything but the magic of his mouth on hers, the way their lips fused together and their tongues danced, as if their bodies had not forgotten a thing.

As if all this time she had simply chained this dragon deep inside of her, but now she'd roused it all over again, fire and fury.

And she could see the edge of that cliff that she'd leaped off once before. She could see how easy it would be to simply throw herself over the edge, allowing this impossible kiss to sweep her away. It would take nothing at all on her part to simply surrender to the storm, to the bright, gleaming dragon that was this passion she'd so deliberately pretended she'd never known— while all the time it had been coiled up inside of her.

But she wasn't the girl she'd been five years ago.

Mila no longer had the luxury to forget who she was.

That had been true five years ago, too. Eventually. It was even more true now. She couldn't block out the simple, undeniable facts that governed her entire existence. She was a queen now, not a princess whose father had given her leave to go out there and find the taste of something normal before it was her turn to take the throne.

She was *the Queen* and this was her palace, and

sooner or later, someone would see them here if they hadn't already. And even though she knew that her staff supported her, and some even adored her, there was always the chance that someone would think a hefty tabloid payment was well worth a simple phone call and the queen's lost trust.

Mila put her hands on his chest, though that was its own mistake. Caius was already too beautiful, too impossibly gorgeous to bear, and that was simply *looking* at him. Touching him was a tragedy and once again, that grief slammed through her.

Because once, long ago and so far away now it seemed like a dream, she had imagined that things could be different.

Once, she had dared let herself *hope*—

But reality had come for her with a vengeance.

She remembered that, too. It was impossible to remember any part of what happened with Caius without remembering how it had ended.

Mila could picture it all too clearly. She had been standing in a hotel room in a haunted city high in the redwoods, staring in complete incomprehension as the guard she had come to view as more of a friend did not smile back at her. The way Noemí always had done before, every time she officially entered Mila's presence on this adventure of theirs, where no one could suspect who Mila was.

Noemí had taken to smiling in place of any curtseys or bows.

That day, her bodyguard had instead dropped into a deep curtsy that had seemed alarmingly out of place in this faraway place that had nothing to do with monarchies or palaces. And seemed absurd given that Noemí had been wearing hiking clothes, adding a kind of madness to the traditional curtsy that had only etched a kind of grotesque hyperreality to the scene.

The King is dead, Noemí had said, her voice gravelly and not like her at all. *Long live the Queen.*

And one of the secrets that Mila held deep in the darkest part of her heart was that for a long, disorienting moment, she had forgotten that *the Queen* was... her.

That the day she'd been preparing for the whole of her life and yet had never wanted to arrive, had come at last.

All this while Caius took a long, hot shower, unaware that everything had changed. That Mila's muchloved father was dead, that she had not had the chance to say goodbye, and that she would now have to mourn him under the searing and inescapable lens of the public.

Many of whom would be looking to their new queen to lead them through.

Their new queen who had done exactly what her father had told her he trusted her *not* to do—and shamed the entire family with an impetuous marriage.

She remembered staring back at Noemí in a silence that seemed to drag on for whole lifetimes, thinking, *What have I done?*

There was all of that pounding through her now, as if it was new, and then there was the reality of Caius. Caius himself, in the flesh. Not the memory of him that had taunted her and tangled itself around her on too many nights she refused to think about come morning.

Caius, who looked down at her when she finally managed to pull away, that mouth of his already moving into its mocking twist, and all that bright, hot fire in his eyes.

Eyes that were a dark, impossible amber ringed in black.

Like he was made of magic.

She had always thought he was.

Not helpful or productive, she scolded herself. "Things are very different than they were back then," Mila managed to say after a moment, grabbing at the remnants of her dignity as best she could.

Instead of letting herself get carried away by his *magic*.

Not that it seemed to affect Caius at all. He reached over and brushed the back of his knuckles over her cheek, as if it was his dearest wish to light her on fire. Then he carefully tucked a piece of hair that should not have fallen from her elaborate updo behind her ear.

"I would not say that *everything* is different," he said, his voice little more than a low rumble.

And to her astonishment and great despair, Mila wanted to cry.

She could feel it rush through her, then rebound as if it meant to drown her where she stood, and for a moment she really did wonder if her knees might buckle.

Because there it was again. The faintest shadow of that sliver of hope she should have known better than to hold on to, all these years later.

The sliver of hope she would have sworn she'd long since extinguished.

She tamped it down, ruthlessly. The way she had learned how to do long ago, because it was that or perish beneath the weight not of her crown, but the piles upon piles of expectations heaped on top of it.

"It is not a simple problem to solve," she told him, when she could be sure she sounded calm. Even. "And I know you disagree. But it has never been simple, no matter how many arguments you mount."

His wizard's gaze gleamed in the dark. "I have made it simple, Mila. You may thank me later. After all, the damage is done. There is only the announcing it."

She'd forgotten too many things, that was the trouble, like how much she wanted to simply *melt* into this man. And she blamed herself for that, too, because ignorance was never something that a queen could allow herself to wallow in, but she'd chosen it in this case. It seemed like valor, all those years ago.

Because she had been reeling from the loss of her father and the loss of this bright magic she'd found with Caius that had seemed as if it might kill her, too.

When she should have known that sooner or later, he would come back. Because people always came back to collect on promises.

Promises she should never have made in the first place.

Mila made herself take one step back, then another, and it felt as excruciatingly painful now as it had that last day. More, maybe, because she'd tried very hard since that day to tell herself that she'd made all of that up. Or, more charitably, that she had been stunned by her father's death and sideswept by all the ramifications of it—all of which had felt very different now that it was more than a theoretical protocol to be discussed while her father was still safely alive.

But no. It just hurt. Everything about Caius was the same agony, no matter how she looked at it.

The difference, she told herself sternly, *is that now you do not have the luxury of showing anyone your feelings,* especially *him.*

Mila pulled herself back into character, though these days she thought it was less a character and more simply who she was. The Queen. Always *the Queen*. She folded her hands in front of her in as regal a manner as possible. She arranged her face into polite impassivity. She managed to look down her nose at him though he still towered over her, and she was not a short woman.

And she pretended that she could not hear that low, mocking sort of laugh of his.

"What announcement do you think we should make?" she inquired with deadly calm and the faintest hint of something almost like interest. Almost, but not quite. "That the man recently seen as the paramour of an old childhood friend is in fact having secret assignations with the Queen? The people will be delighted, I am sure."

"I know this is a long shot," he drawled, in that way he had, with that particular accent of his that was all accents and no accent. And somehow entirely him. "But we could always try the truth."

She shouldn't have mentioned Paula, because now

all she could think about was her friend. Her poor friend, who she had betrayed. There was no other way to look at it. Paula could have had absolutely no idea that Caius was secretly married, much less married to her friend and queen. But Mila knew full well whose arm Caius had arrived on this night.

"The truth is impossible." She almost allowed herself to frown at him. "And now you have made me not only betray myself and my country, but my friend. I think that's a hat trick."

"And to think," Caius replied as if this was all terribly amusing to him, "I'm only getting started."

And that terrible desire, that impossible dragon, was still coiling around inside of her, lighting her up in ways she'd forgotten was possible for her to shine. Just as she'd forgotten what it was like to have someone *touch her* the way he did.

So casually, as if she was a person. As if she was like everyone else, and could be jostled casually, touched carelessly, brushed up against by mistake.

These were things that did not happen to the Queen of Las Sosegadas. These were things that were not allowed to happen. Ever.

These were more things to grieve when she was alone.

"If you'll excuse me," she said, very sternly so that perhaps she would listen to herself, "your date is waiting for me. And likely for you."

"If that's how you want to play it, My Sweet Majesty."

The way he'd used to call her *Princess*. The way he'd

whispered *my princess* while he was deep inside her, filling her so completely she could not imagine how they had ever parted.

Somehow the *My Sweet Majesty* was even...worse.

"I know that you think—" she began, in the sort of placating tone she often used on fractious ministers and unduly contentious politicians.

"I'd be careful with that," he interrupted her, and that, too, was a revelation and a memory all at once. No one else dared speak when she did. No one had in five years, not even her mother. "You don't know what I think. I believe you never did. I would try not to make a fool of myself by pretending otherwise, if I were you."

Mila opted not to inform him that it was impossible for the Queen of Las Sosegadas to be a fool. By definition, tradition, and the odd royal decree.

"An interesting tack you're taking, Caius," she said instead, not letting herself fold. Not even *considering* something like folding, come to that, because it had been a long time since she had ever been required to entertain surrender as a possibility. "I watched a program on this. It's what men these days do, is it not? Perhaps men have always done it. They fear that no woman would ever want them, usually because they are substandard and unworthy. But instead of working to better themselves, they prefer instead to insult women so that they will feel grateful for lowering their standards to men so far beneath them that it's almost amusing that they even try."

And for a moment, then, she simply smiled at him. Not quite sanctimoniously.

"The first thing you should always remember about me," he replied, with that quirk in the corner of his mouth and his eyes entirely too bright, "is that I do not suffer from low self-esteem, a lack of self-confidence, or any of the maladies the men you're talking about do. I am not short, nor am I dull. I am well aware of the way I look and how avidly my company is desired wherever I go. I do not need to play games to get women. I need only exist."

"I see your arrogance has only grown."

"Is it arrogance or simple truth?" He shrugged. "What you need to ask yourself is if you're prepared to deal with the version of me that is no longer interested in keeping your secrets."

She held his gaze as if that little speech did not terrify her, and she did not cower. She did not even blink. After a moment, she inclined her head the faintest bit. "I appreciate you laying out this mission of yours in such stark and unmistakable terms. I will take this opportunity to remind you that I'm not a lost princess on a lost coast any longer. I also know exactly who I am, and I think you'll find that the girl you knew was never anything more than a daydream in the first place."

Mila did not say, *And now I am the Queen, who you would do well to treat more like a potential nightmare.*

She felt it was implied.

"A daydream who had the misfortune to sign legal documents, that is," Caius countered. In that mild way of his that was at complete odds with that blazing fire in his eyes. "Lest you forget."

"Barring that," she said cheerfully, "there are always the dungeons."

And staying here any longer, interacting with him like this, was beginning to feel like an indulgence, so she turned and marched away. She did not wait to see what he would do, because she was the Queen, damn it.

What mattered was what *she* did.

Accordingly, Mila swept off, back into this remote and little-used room. She strode past the guard—sadly not Noemí, who had been rewarded for her extraordinary service and friendship by being made a Baroness of the Realm as one of Mila's first duties, and was now the Minister of Security.

Once she cleared the guard, she raced down the hallway—or her version of racing, since it was undignified to break out into a run. And she checked the clocks standing here and there in all their state as she went. It could not have been more than a handful of minutes that they been together. Ten on the outset. They could not possibly have engaged in anything *too* scandalous in so short a time, and she was in no way disheveled—apart from that one rogue tendril of hair.

Not that she expected that particular guard to betray her, but that was the thing. Anyone could and it wasn't even personal. Because Mila wasn't a *person* to them.

She hurried along to a salon off a different hall, where Paula was waiting. She was seated on a couch, surrounded by all the pictures of Carliz and her growing family that the palace had been able to find, both in Mila's personal collection and from all the press sources.

"I'm so sorry to keep you waiting," she said as she

hurried into the room, waving off the aides that waited unobtrusively, because someone was almost always watching in the palace. "I could lie and tell you that I was swept up in matters of state, but the truth is, I was vetting that date of yours."

Paula laughed. Mila hated herself.

She hadn't even planned that lie. It had simply slipped out. Because she'd had just enough time on her dash over here to think about the fact that Caius could very easily tell his own tales, and start with Paula when he did.

This was who she was now. It was second nature to play elaborate games of chess, whether or not anyone else was playing.

"He is my escort tonight," Paula told her, waving a languid hand. "But he is not a *date*. Can you imagine? Who could possibly take the likes of *Caius Candriano* seriously?"

"I rather thought the point of him was to take him as extremely unseriously as possible," Mila heard herself say. Because, apparently, she couldn't stop.

"It's not that I *wouldn't*," Paula said with another laugh. "If it were the right bad decision I wouldn't hesitate. But I'd sooner jump into bed with a comet than Caius Candriano. I think he would burn a mere mortal to a crisp without even trying."

Mila had never heard a better description of Caius. It was his reputation, certainly—but she rather thought it was simply a primal truth any woman who ventured near him understood at once. In their bones.

And she could feel that comet inside her, burning her alive, even now.

Had she only been pretending, all these years, that she had somehow escaped that fire?

But there was no time to wonder these things. Not now. She turned to the pictures before them, some on the tablet the staff had brought and some printed out. And for another half hour or so, they talked about when they were younger. When they'd stood on opposite sides of ballrooms, Mila exuding duty from every pore while Paula and Carliz had gotten themselves into different sorts of trouble. Paula had always been more about giving her father white hairs and near heart attacks. Carliz had always promised not to embarrass her sister, so she was simply...irrepressible.

Some years Mila had been jealous that they were allowed to behave as they liked, even within the strictures of their class and its expectations. Other years she had felt quite serene in her choices, and her future.

And now here she was, living out that future, only her past—the one she thought she'd hidden away, far from view, where no one could ever find it—had reared its ugly head.

Well, drawled a little voice inside, as if he was still part of her, *not* ugly. *I think you know better than that.*

By the time Paula took her leave, Mila was almost tempted to pretend that she couldn't remember that part of the evening. She said goodbye to her friend and did not accompany her out into the public part of the palace, where she knew Caius would be waiting.

She told herself that discretion was the better part

of valor. That she had nothing at all to fear. That she was not, for that matter, the least bit afraid.

But it was also true that she walked a bit faster to get back to her rooms.

Because once she said good-night to her staff, once she closed her door, she could be *Mila* again until morning.

Just a person. Just herself.

And tonight she had her own mission.

Mila smiled and thanked her staff as they withdrew. She closed the door behind them to her private rooms and stood there a moment, her heart telling truths she didn't want to listen to as it beat much too hard in her chest.

She forced herself to go into the dressing room and take her usual meticulous care of herself, the way she did every night. She had needed help out of the dress, but the rest she could do on her own, and so she did. She changed into what her sister had once called *princess pajamas*. It was a lounging set of the finest, softest cashmere that floated like a whisper over her skin.

And did not in any way remind her of the way Caius had once skimmed his fingers down the length of her—

"Stop it," she chastised herself.

She sat in front of a mirror and took down her hair, brushing it the way she did each night. Her mother had always told her that it was not only her crowning beauty, but would be looked at more than most women's, by virtue of the actual crowns she would be called upon to wear.

Like every other part of the vision that is the Queen,

your hair must gleam with health and vitality, Alondra had declared. Repeatedly, throughout her girlhood.

Health and vitality, Carliz would whisper, twisting her own hair in a knot on the back of her head some years and acting as if she'd never seen a brush.

Mila took off her makeup, cleansed and moisturized her face. And only then, only when she had attended to the physical body of the reigning queen as was her sacred and sovereign duty, did she surrender to that wild and consistent beating thing behind her ribs.

Only then did she dart back into her bedroom, go over to the desk that stood in one far corner, and dig into the back of one of the drawers. She wedged her hand inside, reaching with her fingers until she could push just the right spot.

The drawer pulled out then. And she could pull off the envelope that she had taped there years back. She held the envelope in her hands as if, were she not careful, it might bite her.

Mila took it over to the bed, climbing up into the center of the mattress on this bed that the staff was forever trying to make more ornate and she was always asking them to make simpler. It had four posters, it didn't need a canopy. It had enough pillows, it didn't need a thousand more throw pillows to adorn it. It was already fitted with a soft mattress set to her precise specifications, about which she was quizzed with regularity, lest she spend even one night in discomfort.

And yet she wasn't sure that she'd ever sleep again.

Mila turned the envelope over. Once. Again.

She blew out a breath and then she opened it up, shaking out the content onto the coverlet before her.

Then there was nothing to do but stare down at the delicate gold chain that held only the simple gold ring that she had worn on her finger only once.

Only briefly.

She had thought she might wear it on the chain instead, but had known even before the plane had landed back in Las Sosegadas that she couldn't risk it. It would invite comments at the very least. It would demand speculation.

Mila had hidden it away. And she had not allowed herself to look at it since.

Now, once again, she felt all the same things that had charged around inside of her earlier. That wildfire passion. That intense, impossible connection.

The coiled, golden dragon of the way she longed for him and all the grief and hope and loss that went with it.

There were other things that she could do to handle this situation. She knew that. There was a team in the palace whose job it was to anticipate bad press, or any kind of scandal, and get out ahead of it. She should have been on the phone to them right now.

But Mila didn't pick up her extension.

She stayed where she was, sitting cross-legged on her bed.

She thought of that kiss, that glorious kiss she should not have allowed, and eventually she picked up the gold chain and let the ring dance there on the end of it in the soft light of her bedroom.

Here, only here, where no one would see her and no one would know, she slipped that ring on her finger the way she had years ago.

And for the first time in a long, long while, let the memories wash over as they would, until her mouth tasted of salt and there were no tears left to cry for the man she couldn't have.

The man she shouldn't want.

The man she would have to make herself forget all over again, come morning.

CHAPTER FOUR

A FEW WEEKS later Caius helped himself to a drink at the latest party he had been invited to personally and not as an escort to someone else, looked around yet another crowded ballroom, and congratulated himself on a campaign waged well.

He had single-handedly made Las Sosegadas a premier destination for the very rich and very, *very* bored set, who were always listlessly trailing from yacht to beach, complaining that the dog days of August were tedious in the extreme.

Now they were all cavorting about this pretty little jewel of a mountain kingdom instead, swanning up and down the boulevards and talking in their disaffected drawls as if they'd spent their whole lives holidaying in the kingdom.

"Why broil on the beach when we can be in the mountains instead?" brayed one pouting, supposedly fashionable heiress with a breathlessness she considered her trademark. She waved her cocktail in a manner designed to draw the eyes of her rivals and friends, clustered near the looming pillar. It drew Caius's gaze too, though not for the same reasons. "Besides, I prefer my skin to look like porcelain, not leather."

Hotels were suddenly overbooked all over the kingdom. Housing prices skyrocketed as the sorts of people who liked a fashionable *pied-à-terre* wherever they might find themselves found their way here.

And all Caius had to do was the same thing he always did: wander about these same parties with a smirk on his face. Very much as if he knew something everyone else didn't, the better to drive them all mad.

Because without exception, they all threw themselves into a frenetic competition to pretend they knew exactly what it was that Caius Candriano knew. Whatever it happened to be.

It worked like a charm every time.

That was the power of the mask he'd learned to wear.

It had taken very little time to ingratiate himself with the grand hostesses of the realm, who, naturally, quickly found him indispensable. Was it even a party, they queried each other both in public and private, if Caius was not in attendance?

But he was always in attendance. And he had merited his own invitation shortly after that first party at the palace, followed by every invitation. To everything. It was child's play to make certain that he turned up wherever the Queen was expected.

Sometimes he even got to talk to her, though he made no effort to do so.

Because he knew she expected him to do just that. To *push*. To *encroach*. And the more she expected him to do it, the less he tried.

The glorious result of that was that every night he went out to an event where the Queen was expected, he could feel her temper rise as if she was holding the flame of it to his own skin.

A flame that grew higher and higher each evening he wandered through rooms she was in, pretending he was unaware of her presence. Or better yet, uninterested.

Tonight it was nearing inferno levels, that temper of hers he could feel from clear across the ballroom.

It was possible that he enjoyed it a little too much. Particularly because he knew that he was the only one who could see it. To everyone else, she might as well have been a portrait of herself, stood in her usual place so they could gaze at her from afar.

There was something about that notion that got under his skin, worrying its way deep.

"You should make me your one-man tourism board," he told her later that night when they ended up seated next to each other at the long, sumptuous banquet table.

Not because he had asked for such a manipulation, because he hadn't. He wouldn't. But because the hostess thought she was doing Her Majesty the great favor of bestowing Caius's much-sought-after company upon her. He was the *prize* at these gatherings.

Accordingly, he beamed at Mila and smiled lazily as she committed acts of restrained violence against each and every course that was brought before her.

"We already have a tourism board." She stabbed a succulent shrimp with the tines of her fork. Hard.

"And I was unaware that you had ever worked for a living. Or at all."

"You can be sure, Your Majesty, that I'm very good at..." He waited for her gaze to find his, clearly against her will. He let his smile get even lazier and tinged with wickedness. *"Working."*

He should not have taken so much pleasure in making her react. But he did. There was something about watching the hint of color bloom in her cheeks. About tracking the precise tautness of her lips. Because Caius liked that he could see beneath her mask when no one else seemed aware it was there.

Having seen beneath it, how could he keep himself from trying to pry it off?

Or pretending he might pry it off, anyway. Out here in public, where anyone can see—something he was certain she sat up nights worrying about.

Just so long as you think of me, he'd said when she'd said something like that, though in a way that suggested her worry was cool and rational. Not hot and bothered and *yearning* at four a.m., the way he often was.

"How curious," she said now, in that cool, repressive tone that he could feel directly in his sex. It made him grin. "I was under the impression that you were nothing but a dilettante. Flitting about Europe like an intoxicated butterfly."

"I have also spent rather a lot of time on the West Coast of America," he said, grinning wider at that faint narrowing of her gaze that was as loud as shout to him. "It's the most interesting place. A very rugged sort of beauty. Not nearly as manicured as the Continent can be." He let his smile go guileless. "Have you been? On a state visit, perhaps?"

She did not dignify that with either a glare or a reply. She turned to the person on her other side instead, engaging the older woman in what sounded like a very dull discussion of economic programs that had failed to achieve their stated goals.

When the next course came, she returned her attention to Caius with a baleful sort of glare. Because, he knew, she would have continued to ignore him all night but that would elicit as much comment—maybe more. She was expected to divide the favor of her notice equally and Mila was scrupulous when it came to managing the expectations put upon her.

He would have made a terrible queen, he had often thought.

"How long do you intend to grace the kingdom with your presence?" she asked.

"I had originally thought to stay only a day or so." He leaned back in his chair so he could *lounge* at her, boneless and unfazed by her regal consequence, which was not strictly polite. But then again, he was already the darling of society here, and everywhere. He was allowed leeway and what was the point of such allowances if he couldn't take advantage of it. "I am looking into buying some property here."

"Whatever for?"

"Surely your kingdom's charms advertise themselves, Your Majesty."

"I have always found the charms of the kingdom profound. It is the kind of place that becomes a part of a person's soul." That smile of hers flashed then, and he saw how easily she could make it a weapon. She aimed it straight at him. Then held it to his throat. "Are you in possession of one of those?"

Caius should not have found himself disarmed. So easily.

But he was.

Later, maybe, he would piece together what happened just then. That flash of the girl he remembered there in that gleaming gaze of hers, for only him to see. And the joy of it, that unexpected attack.

She'd enjoyed it, and so he had, too.

"I doubt I have ever known the touch of a soul," he answered honestly. And quite without meaning to. "Yet somehow I muddle along."

"Pretending, is that it?" Mila was no longer stabbing at her food. And though he knew better than to indulge this in public, he could feel the current between them then, blocking out everything else. When that was nothing but dangerous. "Just preening in the dead center of whatever stage you can find? Playing whatever role will get you whatever it is you want in that moment?"

He forgot himself entirely. "I thought that was your role. Your entire objective is to disappear until you become your own statue, is it not?"

And they were both lucky, he thought, that the hostess chose that precise moment to surge to her feet and start making proclamations in the form of a deferential speech, so that no one heard him.

But Mila did.

There were cheers all around, applause and toasts, but their gazes seemed tangled together with too many ghosts in between.

Until she tore her gaze away and cooled back into her preferred state of flesh become stone, the perfect queen.

The next morning, he woke before dawn, as was his custom. Though he went to great lengths not to let that sort of thing get out. It would ruin his reputation as a debauched hedonist entirely.

Caius slipped out of his hotel before the sun's rays fully penetrated the grand valley. He went on a long, hard run, out there beside the sparkling alpine water of the Royal Lake.

But no matter how many kilometers he ran, or how fast he ran them, he couldn't outrun Mila.

And it was only when he was out there with his legs pumping, his heart pounding, and his breath coming hard and fast to remind him that he was alive, that he accepted the fact that seeing her like this—all the time, but never close enough to touch, not really—was perhaps backfiring.

Because the truth was that he'd expected that he would have one or two interactions with her and no longer find it necessary to even play these games. Or he had hoped. He had assumed that the girl he had known was the part she'd played, and that there would be no trace of her in the dauntingly serene *Queen Emilia*.

Instead, he could see the girl he'd known peering out of the Queen's eyes sometimes. Every time her cheeks flushed, but only slightly. Every time there was that snap of temper in her gaze that no one else seemed to notice.

He could see her there, peering out. Reminding him that he hadn't made her up. That she had existed all this time. She was *just there*, just out of reach.

With only the small matter of a throne and a crown between them.

He ran for hours and when he made it back to his hotel, he wasn't surprised to find all kinds of messages on his mobile. He ignored them. And when the phone rang as he stood there, gulping down water and staring out the window at the palace that rose on the hill, he almost ignored it.

But that would only make call *more*.

"Caius," said his sister when he answered, "what in the world are you doing? Since when do you hunker down in one place like this? I've never known you to turn your back on your vagabond ways. It's chilling."

"Good morning, Lavinia," Caius replied mildly. "That's a bit dramatic, don't you think? It's been a few weeks. Not years."

"You once told me that anything more than a long weekend in a place was dangerous. Roots might spring up when you least expected it and hold you there forever."

"That sounds like teenage poetry and I, happily, never wrote such trash."

Though he had almost certainly said exactly that when he was an adolescent. It sounded like him.

Lavinia laughed at that, because the two of them

were the only members of their sprawling, complicated, maddening family who had always gotten on. Probably because they had endured such a nomadic existence when they were young, forever being dragged from one hotel to the next, in service to their mother's bottomless need for attention.

In those days, the Countess—as his mother preferred to be known, though her pretensions to the title were questionable at best—had in fact been homeless. But that was not a word anyone used when the person in question was of a certain social strata.

Or when she was a particular strain of attractiveness. The right width. The right way of dressing. The right friends, the right parties, the right way of manipulating events until she got what she wanted.

Another word for his mother was *grifter*, but it was so impolite to say such things out loud.

Along with other words like *narcissist*. *Alcoholic*. *Countess* was easier.

"I know why you're calling me," Caius said. "I would have thought my not answering was its own clear message."

Lavinia laughed again. "The Countess is becoming alarmingly tedious about this. She refuses to ask you herself, but she will be absolutely devastated if you don't come to this wedding of hers."

"I was at her last five weddings. Speaking of tedium."

"She claims this one is different."

"She always does," he reminded his sister. "And why

are *you* accepting her calls? Last I heard, you vowed not to be a party to this nonsense any longer."

"Someone has to answer her calls," his sister said, with the sort of defeated sigh he recognized only too well. Having made that sound himself more than he cared to recall.

He could hear some city or other in the background of wherever she was. Honking horns, spirited snatches of conversation. Whole lives that were conducted without the slightest interest in what one deranged woman they happened to be related to was or wasn't doing.

"That is false," he told his sister. "Someone always *does* answer her calls, but that doesn't mean you need to be that person, Lavi." He pronounced it *Lovey*, as he had since they were small. An unfair weapon then and now. "Besides, she has other children."

"None of them would dare call you," Lavinia said with a cackle. "They are far too protective of their own skins. I find it absolutely hilarious that the papers are filled with all the stories of *'Caius Candriano, the most beloved and delightful guest at every society event,'* but anyone who knows you knows the truth. You're a holy terror."

"There is absolutely no difference in my behavior anywhere I go," Caius told her with great dignity. He took another swig of his water, still glaring out at that palace. "I can't help it if our family doesn't like the way I tell a truth."

"Tell yourself whatever you need to," Lavinia said with an audible eye roll. "The Countess is getting married again, whether we like it or not. I don't even know what number it is, because I have chosen not to process the final tally. As it so often changes."

"I cannot for the life of me understand why you're engaging with this, Lavi."

But she continued as if he hadn't spoken. "It would be one thing if you were simply unreachable, forever here, forever there. But it seems as if you've settled in this place. You're in the papers every day. How would it look if you couldn't come to your own mother's wedding?"

"One can only hope it will be seen as a complete lack of interest in a very boring subject, as we all know there will be another wedding to attend." Caius rubbed his hand over his face but the palace was still there, looming, when he opened his eyes again. Mila might as well have been on the other side of the glass, staring him down with that look of hers, unknowable and imperious at once.

"Have you met him?" Lavinia asked.

"I don't need to meet him."

"Anyway, Caius," she said in the resigned tone of one who is forced to soldier on despite unforeseen and obnoxious resistance, "it will hurt her feelings if you don't make an appearance."

"You and I both know that the Countess does not have any feelings."

"Forgive me." This time the sigh was aggrieved and aimed directly at him. "What I meant to say is that you are by far her most famous offspring. She will be humiliated and outraged if you don't turn up the way she wants. You know how she gets when that happens."

"Goodbye Lavinia," Caius said in the same mild voice he'd been using all along, because he knew it would annoy her. "Stop doing her dirty work."

And he could hear his laughing as he rang off.

He stayed where he was for a moment, frowning down at his mobile and wondering if he should add insult to injury and give his father a call. Just to see how badly the old man was messing up his life these days, what with his addictions to fast cars, too much gambling, and making a mockery of his family's once good name.

It was enough to give a man a complex, if Caius was the kind of man who allowed himself such things. But that was another thing that had never been allowed when he was a child. Only his mother was permitted feelings.

And hers were operatic.

He and Lavinia were the oldest of his mother's five children. Each of them was the product of a different father and all of those fathers also had other children elsewhere. This had led to what Caius liked to call the dark comedy of family events, not that anything was ever very funny. But because the Countess had kept Caius and Lavinia with her for the longest period of time—there being at least ten years between Caius and the next in line, which had led to all kinds of bonding between him and his older sister—the two of them had always considered themselves their own family.

As for the rest, he sometimes had to do a bit of research on his Wikipedia page to figure out all the ins and outs of who he was related to.

If asked in public, he liked to make a joke of it. There were all kinds of unflattering terms to describe a woman like his mother, who was forever jumping from one man to the next and having babies many of them as possible, so that they were forced to feel responsible for her forever. There were many ways to describe the kind of woman who made her living that way, but because the Countess came with a pedigree and had a claim to exiled royalty of one form or another, no one ever used those terms. No one would dare.

The fact that she was a cruel, vain, vicious woman seemed to trouble absolutely no one at all. She wandered from man to man, dragging her kids along as props and abandoning them to hotel staff when she bored of them, or might be asked to *parent* in some way. She threw them into schools then yanked them out again, without caring at all how they might feel about it—and woe betide anyone if they complained or so much as drew her attention when she was not in the mood to remember their existence.

She had left Caius on his own in a hotel room in Berlin once for *bothering* her. She'd sent for him ten days later, and had punished him for the inconvenience. He had been eight.

Caius had hated every moment of his childhood.

But he had made that same kind of lifestyle his entire personality as he grew older. He was a man who followed his limbs whoever they took him. He had not allowed himself to stop and attempt to fix his childhood, because if he did, that might indicate that it needed that fixing in the first place. That *he* did.

And he had decided at some point in his adolescence that he was perfect as he was.

There was absolutely no need to change a thing.

One significant benefit of growing up the way he had was that he could charm anyone. He'd had to do it more times than he could recall—at his mother's command or to get out of a tricky situation—and now he chose to use that skill all the time. He could charm anyone. He could fit in anywhere. He could be anything to anyone, and he had taken pride in that.

Until Mila.

And that was the part he couldn't forgive, not even after all this time. She had looked at him as if she could see who he *really* was. Not the person he pretended to be. Not the role he'd been playing all his life.

She had spent only those few months with him and she had been a revelation.

And all of it was a lie.

Maybe, he thought as he looked out the window at her palace, he shouldn't blame her for that. Maybe it was his fault for imagining that what had happened between them could be real once they let the world back in. Because he really should have known better. He had always prided himself on being a realist.

And then one look at her and it was as if he'd never learned a thing.

Maybe he needed to accept that even though he'd vowed that he would never marry—so he could never divorce, much less as many times as his parents had—he had gone ahead and done it anyway.

And maybe he really should go to his mother's latest wedding, where he would learn her husband's name just in time for them to separate, because it might teach him a valuable lesson that he'd never wanted to learn.

He was exactly the same as everyone else in his tangled and embarrassing family tree. He was certainly no better than the rest of them.

It had been madness to think so.

Caius stared out at the palace where Mila was, there and yet gone the way he should have known she always was and ever would be, and let out a kind of groan that seemed to come from deep in his bones.

He would give her that divorce. He should have done it long ago.

Then he would leave this pretty kingdom of hers and he would never come back. He would never stay put anywhere, ever again, because that was what he knew. That was who he was.

Slow down and your devils can find you, his mother had liked to say when she was drunk. *You'll meet yours soon enough, my boy. You* are *one*.

And he thought that really, he should never have imagined that he could be a different kind of man than the one the Countess had raised.

Just a pretty face, a charming smile, and the good sense to never overstay his welcome.

That night, he dressed exquisitely. Everywhere he went in the ballroom *du jour* women watched him, laying down palm fronds with their covetous gazes.

Caius knew he was resplendent. Just as he knew Mila would be able to see him even if he wasn't, the moment she entered the gala.

He would simply have to take comfort in the fact that she would read about him in the tabloids forever. And that he would do the same.

It was more than some people had, but at least he could make sure she would never forget him.

"Have you heard?" one of his companions asked him. When he only looked at her and shook his head, she clapped her hands together. "The Queen is looking for a husband at last. *Everyone* is talking about it."

"Is she indeed."

And the woman beside him saw only his charm. His smile. Not the chasm that had opened wide beneath him and was filled with sharp teeth that were now sinking into him, deep.

"Maybe you should apply for the position," the woman said, laughing shrilly. She even put her hand on his arm, as if they were friends. As if he was alive. "Wouldn't that be a laugh? Can you imagine *King Caius*?"

But that was going to be a problem, he thought, his gaze on Her Majesty as she entered the room in a sweep of deep lavender and gray serenity.

Because it turned out, he could imagine *King Caius*. Vividly.

CHAPTER FIVE

"COULD YOU PLEASE tell me why it is," Mila said in an undertone to her mother, her perfect smile never wavering, "that every man on the palace grounds who does not work here appears to be looking at me?"

"You are the Queen of Las Sosegadas. Pray, where else should they look?"

"They are looking at me less like I am their beloved sovereign and more as if I am a piece of meat hanging in a marketplace," Mila replied, bestowing her smile upon a group of women, who did not make her want to check to see if she'd accidentally walked out of her dress before exiting the palace. "And what is more, I believe you know it."

Beside her, Alondra was gazing serenely about, with an air of satisfaction that boded ill. "Your Majesty, forgive me, but I am unaware of any time you have spent in any marketplaces. Particularly marketplaces that have raw meat hanging on display."

Mila was far too well trained to give her mother the look that comment deserved. "If I'm not mistaken, old Lord Stefano, who I believed entirely too withered and ancient for such sport, licked his lips in my direction."

Alondra sniffed, gazing censoriously in Lord Stefano's general direction. "How terribly uncouth."

They continued walking at the usual sedate pace that Mila had been told her entire life was the appropriate speed at which a queen should cover ground. Sometimes, like today, every muscle inside her body fairly *hummed* with the need to do something...explosive.

That didn't mean blowing up her life, the way she would have done if she'd returned home from the far reaches of America to announce to all and sundry at her father's funeral that she had taken the notably unsuitable Caius Candriano as her husband. Not just as her husband, but as the future king.

That was not the sort of explosiveness she meant. She had no intention of stumbling over that sort of landmine. She wasn't sure she knew how she'd done it in the first place.

What she thought sometimes was that it might be quite pleasant indeed to take up an actual sport of some kind. She had always been discouraged from such pursuits because, her mother had told her icily years ago, no one wished to see the future Queen heaving about on a court in a red-faced sweat.

An image so horrifying that Mila wasn't sure she'd allowed herself to perspire for years afterward.

On days like today, however, she rather thought that whacking something with a racket sounded like nothing short of a delight. Especially when she thought about Caius—something she forbade herself and yet she found herself doing it anyway—who had taken up...lurking.

If anyone that dramatically beautiful and attention-getting could be said to lurk, that was.

Today was an annual late-summer event in the kingdom. The Royal Gardens were opened to the public once in spring, once at the end of summer, and once not long before Christmas when the gardens were done over into a veritable pageant of a Christmas card. Mila was currently doing her usual August promenade from the sweeping steps of the palace down the long, paved walk that cut through the heart of the gardens and allowed for press pictures, meet-and-greets, and the like.

But unlike all the balls she threw and attended throughout the season, this was the sort of event that was open to the entire kingdom. Not simply the aristocracy and the usual touring heirs to this and scions of that, where a certain level of snobbish hierarchy was expected.

These were the three events a year where, once her initial promenade was finished, she could simply… wander as she liked. She could talk to her subjects more freely when she encountered them. She did not have to work as hard on seeming approachable and relatable because, for once, she did not have to exude them through a smile. She could simply *be* those things one-on-one.

Normally she loved everything about the Garden Galas. But today she could not say that she liked the way a great number of the particularly high in the instep were looking at her. Something that did not go away as they walked.

"This is not the first time I've noticed this, Mother,"

Mila said from beneath another smile. "It's been going on for at least a week. What have you done?"

"I have done nothing at all, Your Majesty, except what I have always done. Which is to adhere, as ever, to your every stated wish."

Mila nearly forgot herself and laughed. "That has a rather ominous ring."

A sideways glance from the Queen Mother indicated that it was finally occurring to her that Mila was losing her patience. She cleared her throat, something she managed to make sound delicate. "It was at one of our private dinners the other week. You were brooding down at your game hen and said that you were thinking of marrying."

Mila actually did laugh at that, and had to cover it by pretending that she was *that* engaged in the antics of a set of squealing children who stood along the path. But as soon as they walked past she actually turned her whole head and pinned her mother with a glare, and she wasn't even certain she managed to keep a smile on her face while she did it.

"I am absolutely certain I said no such thing."

Her mother looked startled. But the Queen Dowager Alondra was made of nothing soft, inside or out. She lifted her chin and barreled forth the way she always did. "You may not have used those words, I grant you. We were talking of your sister. And how impossible it seemed that Carliz would ever settle down. How can you not recall this?"

"I said that life is endlessly surprising." Mila's voice was quiet, but she knew her mother did not mistake the hint of steel in it. "That it was impossible to say what the next turn of the season might bring. We were speaking of *Carliz*, Mother."

"And then Your Majesty said, and I quote, *'The mistake we make is believing anything can be set in stone.'*"

Alondra looked at her in triumph.

Mila gazed back. "I am waiting in breathless anticipation to see how you interpreted that to mean that I would like to walk about my kingdom being slobbered over by every man who dares look at me. Truly. I cannot wait."

"There has only ever been one thing you have declared set in stone," her mother said primly. "I merely whispered in a few ears that perhaps, after all this time, the stone has begun to shift."

Mila fumed for the rest of what was normally her happy promenade.

When it was finished, she took the requisite photos with the gardening team, shook the hands of expected dignitaries, met the people who had been selected to receive her special notice this day, and then lost no time setting off for her wander when it was all done.

But she didn't follow her normal route. Usually she made her way through the summer flowers, happening into conversations as she found them, with whoever she discovered along the way. It was one of her favorite things to do.

Today, however, she headed for the maze.

Unlike some garden mazes that were built as follies and design elements and would not have confused a toddler, the palace maze here had been the brainchild of one of the kingdom's darker figures. Prince Clemente had poured his animosity for his long-lived and famously unpleasant father into this particular creation on the palace grounds, where it was said he preferred to tarry so as to avoid the intrigue of the royal court as much as possible.

Much of the maze was made of tall evergreens that did not fade away with the seasons at this elevation, but continued to stand tall and impenetrable all winter. Its narrow little passages twisted this way and that as it rambled about in its dizzying manner. It was impossible to see into it from above, and entirely too easy to get lost in it on the ground. Some even claimed it was haunted, and the routes to the center some believed did not exist changed at the whim of the maze itself.

But for Mila, the maze had always been a place of refuge.

Because of its reputation, most people avoided it, so filled was it with superstition and all the whispered stories of dark things that might have happened within it.

What that meant, she knew from experience, was that very few people braved the narrow, thorny, gnarled little pathways. Most people never made it to the center. But she knew where it was—she could get there blindfolded—and she headed there now.

And the farther she moved away from the sound of all of those voices—all of that polite laughter, the buzz of gossip, speculation, and apparently, now, talk of marriage—she felt more and more like *herself*.

Like the Mila she got to be when she closed the door to her bedroom each night.

The Mila she was when Caius looked at her and the world fell away.

The farther she went, the better it felt, so she actually let herself move faster, then faster still, until she was running flat out.

Until she was breaking a damned sweat.

As if she was just a woman. Just a human being, hurtling unseen and yet protected by these hedges. Just out here running on a pretty summer day because it felt good to run. Using her body because it was hers. Because she wasn't simply a figure stamped on the side of a coin. She breathed. She bled.

Every once in a while, she even wept.

And for a few months, long ago, she had let herself feel every single thing a human could. Every beautifully mortal sensation, on every centimeter of her body, and she hadn't cared what she looked like while it was happening. She had spared not one thought for the sounds she made or the position of her lips on her face.

She had been *alive* in a way she hadn't been before or since.

Mila ran faster and faster, filled with a kind of mad, desperate exultation.

She burst into the center of the maze at last, skidding to a stop in the sweet-scented grove and blowing out a long breath that seemed to take from every part of her. As if it was scooping out everything inside of her, all those old ghosts and long-held fears and regrets, and releasing them all into the sacred geometry of this hidden place.

Here in the center, the grim hedges gave way to flowering trees. They cast shade, dancing over the sparkling pool that gleamed there in the sunshine. As if that long-ago crown prince, despite his dark feelings for everything within the palace, had been unable to prevent himself from showing his soft center to the very few people who ever made it here.

Mila was panting a bit as she walked to the edge of the pool. She gazed down at it, looking less for her reflection and more for the sense that she could, if she wished, be the woman she had only ever been in a real sense for a scant few months on the other side of the world.

I want to feel as if I chose *not to be her*, she thought fiercely.

Then she said it out loud. "I chose to come home. I chose to be Queen. I *chose* this."

Her dress felt heavy all around her after running as she had in it, but she didn't mind. Because for once, for a moment, she felt light. Airy.

And the same old dark thoughts pressed in, but she ignored them. Here, now, she shoved them aside.

Because she did not need to spend more time litigating her own behavior. Or her choices. That was in a past she could not change.

She had *chosen* to marry Caius long ago in a civil ceremony on a beach during a golden sunset, presided over by stranger who had never heard of either one of them.

And she had kissed Caius here in her own palace, though she certainly knew better. She could pretend that he had *stolen* that kiss, as if she had been a piece of candy in a store somewhere that someone could palm on their way out the door. Instead of what she actually had been, a grown woman, a literal queen, who had known exactly what he intended to do and had let him do it.

If she was honest, she had wanted him to do it.

Mila could lecture herself about what she owed her country and do a few more rounds about what her duty was and what she owed her family and her people and the very ground she stood upon, but not today.

Not here, where no one could see her.

Because this was the only place on the palace grounds where she ever felt like that anonymous girl she'd been for only those very few months of her life.

That was the gift her father given her before his death. That was the magic he had bestowed upon her.

It is too dangerous, she had said at once when he'd called her into the bedchamber where he'd spent his last days. She had sat on the edge of the bed as indicated when he'd inclined his head toward the mattress and had frowned at him. All the while ignoring that fluttering, leaping thing inside her at the very idea. *What if I were to be kidnapped? What if I were to get myself into trouble? It would reflect badly on you and the whole kingdom.*

You will not travel with an entourage, he had said quietly. *Only one guard who has been training for the position. She will be tasked to look and act the part of a friend. The two of you will fly commercial. You will drive a rental car, eat in regular restaurants, sleep in unsecured hotels, and at no point will you do a single thing that would make anyone imagine you are in fact the Crown Princess of a royal house.*

That fluttering thing was threatening to take her over, but she had learned her lessons well. But...

The King had reached over and rested his hand on her leg. *My father sent me off to do the same thing when I was about your age. It was his belief that no one can fully commit themselves to this life without experiencing a different one, however briefly.*

But the risk... She'd tried again.

I trust you, Mila, he had said simply. *I trust you to take care of my kingdom when I am gone, you know this. But I trust you to take care of yourself, as well. I'm certain you possess discernment enough to track your own course and the wisdom to do so in a way that shames neither you, this family, nor the crown.*

He had paused as if he'd expected her to mount another argument, but she couldn't.

This is the greatest gift I could give you, he'd said then. *A small window of anonymity before you become, as you inevitably will, public property in almost every way.*

She had wanted to cry, though she hadn't.

And then she had gone and planned not simply a trip, the way many did for gap years and the like. Mila had planned a mission. She had reveled in the challenge. She'd had Noemí collect the items they would need from shops where normal people went. Things the Crown Princess of Las Sosegadas would never possess.

When it was time, they had snuck out of the palace under cover of night, and Mila had laughed as they'd crossed the border. That had the last time someone had recognized the name on her passport. After that, even if there was a second look, she was instantly dismissed.

Because it beggared belief that a woman with the name Emilia Christiana de Las Sosegadas could possibly have anything to do with a princess or a crown far off in the mountains between Spain and France.

They had spent two months wandering where they liked, through cities Mila had never had the opportunity to explore on her own, before they decided to take that particular guided hike through a dangerous stretch of the Pacific Crest Trail.

Nothing but nature for weeks, Noemí had said. *Hard to be more anonymous than that.*

That was where Mila had finally met Caius, who she had certainly heard of before. And had possibly even seen at some or other event, though they had never interacted.

Someone had likely seen to it that they never crossed paths.

She could admit that she hadn't known whether to be thrilled or disappointed that he hadn't seemed to recognize her at all.

It was only later, when they had been telling each other truths at last, that he'd admitted that he'd known who she was at once. That he had hoped that if he didn't indicate that he knew who she was, she wouldn't say anything either, and none of the others in their group would be any the wiser. None would know that they were in the presence of two extremely famous people in a place no one would think to look for them.

They had spent the last few months of her six-month adventure completely inseparable. To the point where Noemí had allowed them time to themselves, and Mila had not thought twice about taking it.

It was something she had never had before. Something it had not occurred to her to treasure—though she knew, even then, that she would miss it. For days on end she got to feel what it was like to have no eyes on her at all save those she loved, from morning until night.

It was like a prayer she hadn't known she needed answered.

And it was only here in this quiet, secluded place where no one knew she liked to come to see her real face in a pool no one else could critique, and breathe her own breaths with any expression on her face she liked, that she could let herself remember those months.

Really, truly remember them.

And that person she'd been then, when she'd been as close to free as she'd ever come.

It wasn't the freedom she missed, Mila knew. It was the way she'd felt in her own skin. Invincible. Entirely herself.

Not subject to any whim but her own.

Her fist clenched involuntarily, as if she was still holding the ring he'd given her. As if she hadn't carefully tucked it away again, back behind the desk drawer, vowing not to give in to the urge to take it out again.

Vowing she would leave it there for future generations to wonder over when they found it, a mystery forever unsolved.

She stayed there until her breathing slowed. She smoothed down her dress and composed her features. Only then was she ready to be *the Queen* again. Only then did she turn, shoulders straightened, to head back out and face the music.

"The music is your life," she said under her breath. "You love your life."

But before she could launch into a series of fierce affirmations to remind herself of why that was true, she stopped.

Because he was there.

He was *right there* and there was no telling how long he'd been there.

Caius stood in the opening to the hidden central grove, seeming to gleam like sunshine though he stood in the shade. He was dressed like the perfect male fantasy of a garden party. All creams and whites, yet slightly rumpled, as if he was far too uncontained, too languidly dangerous, to suit such elegance.

He didn't say a word.

She didn't ask him how he had managed to follow her through the maze or if he'd simply found his own way. He was capable of either, she knew.

"I suspect you heard that I'm looking for a husband," she said, because he would have to have heard. And there was that certain glinting thing in his gaze that made everything in her...*tremble.* "Never fear. I'm not planning to set off on a bigamist excursion. That is the precise opposite of anything I would ever be tempted to do."

Caius still did not say anything.

And Mila had spent more time that she would like to admit thinking about this man in the years since those months together. Every time she'd seen his picture in a tabloid, with the inevitably stunning women falling all over him in front of a cameras, she'd imagined what it would be like for the two of them. Against her will, she'd let the images of him and all of them into her head.

Because she knew. All of that fire. All of that lazy intent.

Mila knew what he could do. And how he did it.

He drifted farther into the small grove, seeming to both take it all in and yet never shift his gaze from her at the same time. He kept his hands thrust deep in his pockets, which made him look slouchy and disreputable, and seemed nothing more than an extension of that little curve that was always in the corner of his mouth.

"So this is where you come," he said in that low voice of his that seemed to hum inside her on a frequency all its own. "Where you can simply be Mila."

He might as well have taken out a stun gun and fired it at her. It seemed to hit her with the force of that kind of weapon, dialed up to the highest possible voltage. She hissed in a shocked breath.

"There is no *Mila* to be, simply or otherwise," she told him, though it felt like a sacrilege, here beside the pool. For now she could see not her reflection, but theirs. Together, like a memory.

Like a warning, she tried to tell herself.

"No?" he asked, but indulgently. As if he knew better. "Not anywhere?"

"There is less and less Mila every day," she told him quietly. "That's a good thing. There is no room for anything else but the Queen. Anything that is not the Queen is a distraction."

"You get to be human, you know." And he did not sound indulgent then. It was much more intense than that. Or maybe it was the way he looked at her with that wizard's gaze. "Because you are actually human, Mila. All the palaces and crowns and fancy dresses in the world can't change that."

It was so close to her usual line of thought when she was here she wanted to cry. And that made her want to throw something at him, because queens did not cry. Not in the light of day. Not where anyone could witness that sort of breakdown.

She felt her fists clench again and had to stop herself from looking down at her left hand to see if that circle of gold was there. She knew it wasn't. She *knew* it wasn't, and yet still, she glanced.

The worst part was that he did, too.

"What do you *want*, Caius?" she asked. *Again.* "If it is something I can give you, I will. But I can't allow this to keep happening. I can't allow myself to be fractured like this. It serves no one. Like it or not, being *the Queen* is my role on this earth, no matter how human I am. I'm here to serve the people of his kingdom, irrespective of any wants or needs or dreams. Much less any ill-advised adventures I might have had in a different lifetime."

"It was this lifetime, Mila." His voice was gravel then. His eyes were fire. "I was there."

She shook her head. "Neither one of us was really there. It was a dream. A beautiful dream, but we should have let it stay just that. A *dream*."

She thought he would argue. Instead, he bent down and found a pebble, then tossed it across the smooth surface of the water with an easy flick of his wrist. Together they counted the skips.

The pebble bounced five times, then sank.

He swallowed, then spoke without looking at her. As if the ripples on the pool were too fascinating to turn away from. "I heard that after this flower show—"

"It is the August Garden Gala," she interjected coolly. "A great favorite of the people."

Caius acknowledged that with the faintest crook of one brow. "After this, I am told you retreat for the month of September."

"I do indeed." Mila looked back over her shoulder to where the palace rose in the distance. It seemed so far away, here by the pool. "It's a place called, creatively enough, the September House. And it is not exactly the stately affair some might imagine. It is quite wild. And very remote. The sovereign generally spends some time there at least once a season." She tried to aim her usual public smile at him, but it felt strange on her mouth. Stiff and unwieldy. "A time for reflection, some say.

My father liked to hunt. His father was a keen cross-country skier."

"What do you do?"

She found herself turning to face him. And it was different here, where there was no one watching. When it wasn't the middle of the night and she was still reeling from the shock of seeing him at all.

When Mila looked up at him, she knew better than to allow herself to yearn for things she couldn't have. She found herself wishing against wish that she could be someone else.

Only for a moment. Another stolen span of time.

"I do very little," she told him, hoping her wishes did not show on her face. "There's a daily call with certain ministers, of course, and a government to run. Other than that, I am left to my own devices."

When Caius only gazed back at her as if he truly wanted to know, as if he was still the man she had considered her only truly safe space on earth, if only briefly, she sighed a little. "At first I took my mother and my sister with me when I went. But I stopped that after the first time. I didn't want to be anything while I was there. Not a queen. Not a daughter. Not even a sister, which I would say is the easiest role of the three." She lifted a shoulder and let it drop. "I just wander about as if I'm anyone. As if I'm no one. I cook my own meals. I clean up after myself. Doesn't that sound silly, that a grown woman could find these things transcendent? Transformative?"

"Not at all," he said, and there was too much memory in his voice then. Too much of the Caius she'd loved so recklessly, so heedlessly, so fast. "I was there the first time you let yourself be anyone and no one. I'm glad to know you still do it."

In the distance, she heard a swell of laughter on the breeze. It was the waning days of August now. And the summer was always stuffed full of events, so that she usually couldn't wait to set off to the September House.

But she knew that this year would be different. Because she knew no matter when she went, she would take this aching thing inside of her along with her.

"I did hear that you planned to start looking for a husband," he confessed, maybe to that ache. Maybe to the memories they shared. "I was incensed."

"Let me guess. You assumed I was throwing down the gauntlet. Directly at you."

"Something like that." It was the way he looked at her, the way no one else ever did or ever would. As if he saw the things she worked so diligently to hide. It was the way he saw *Mila* first, always, and had to look for *the Queen*, when for everyone else she knew—including herself—it was the opposite. It was the way he seemed to have no notion of the reverence he was meant to show in her presence. All the deference he was meant to display. Not Caius. He only reached out and brushed something from her cheek as if she could just…*be touched* like that. Then his mouth curved, likely because he could feel the same heat that she did. "I set about plotting how best to disrupt this process immediately."

She laughed, despite herself. And the glory was, she didn't have to try to hide it. "How marvelous. I can't decide if I think you would go for a big, splashy sort of disruption, for maximum scandal and rippling aftereffects. Or if you were looking for something more stealthy, for more of a seismic, earthquake effect."

There was a flash of his teeth and that smile of his he used far more rarely than people thought. They always remembered him smiling, laughing, but in reality, it was usually that smirk. He was witty, not funny. There was a difference.

And when it came to Caius, all of it was sharpened to a point and wielded with precision.

"I haven't decided yet," he told her, still smiling. "It was all going to depend on what lies you told me."

"And now?" Her hands ached with the effort of keeping them to herself. "Have you decided my fate?"

"Before I heard about your dating plans, I had intended to divorce you." But he was still standing so close to her. He found a tendril of her hair and was wrapping it, ever so slowly, around and around one finger. "I was going to tell you that I would sign whatever papers you needed signed, so that we could dissolve the legalities as if they had never occurred in the first place."

"I think," she whispered, "that you don't actually know what you want, Caius."

He tugged the bit of hair he had wrapped around his finger and they both made the faintest noise, as if they were singing in a kind of harmony.

Mila knew that harmony. It was that ache inside of her. It was that grief.

But it was less and less like grief the longer they

gazed at each other like this. It shifted. It became that long, lingering, golden heat.

She recognized it. The way it wound around and around inside of her. The way it lit her on fire and the flames seemed to reach every part of her, only to settle between her legs. The way it made her soft and needy in an instant.

Oh, yes. She remembered the song too well.

"I have always known exactly what I want, Mila," Caius told her.

"You only want me because you know that you can never truly have me," she replied, and she hardly knew where those words were coming from. But they felt true as she said them. And she wasn't hurling them out. She wasn't even upset. If anything, it was another part of that same golden heat. The part of her that grieved for having to give him up. Again. And always. No matter what she wanted. "It's much easier to blame it all on me, isn't it? Then we don't have to ask ourselves what you might have done to change the landscape." He stared back at her, something like affront in his gaze, or perhaps all that magic was laced with a kind of acknowledgment she doubted either one of them wished to face, or speak out loud. "You could have made yourself into a paragon, Caius. A saint among men."

"What would be the point?" he returned, and he didn't sound intense or furious, either. "Each and every strand of my bloodline is shiny in its way, but altogether? It's a whole lot of mud. And we know you can't have that."

"Just remember that you get to make choices. I am

bound to fulfill my duty. No one ever said it would be *pleasant*, I assure you."

He let out a breath, or maybe it was a curse too soft to hear. "What's the point of having all this power, Mila, if you only wield it to make yourself miserable?"

"What are my options?" She leaned in close, because that felt like power. Then she reached up so she could set a palm on each side of his jaw, holding that beautiful face fast between them. And that felt even better, even if it hurt. "This was always better as a dream, Caius. The more we do this, the more we tarnish it. Is that really what you want?"

She felt his hands cover hers, but all she could *see* was the way he looked at her. The way he had always looked at her.

As if their hearts beat in the same rhythm, even now.

"So which is it?" she asked him, keeping her gaze trained on his. "Will you expose me to all of my people, making them all question my judgment forever? Will you attempt to seduce me so you can cause a new scandal in real time? Or will you simply say goodbye, and let us both remember what this was fondly?"

Mila didn't know how she managed to say that so calmly, when inside, she felt ravaged. She felt torn into ragged little pieces, but that didn't matter. That had never mattered. She could rip her heart out of her chest and hurl it out of the highest window in the palace, and it still wouldn't matter. She would still be *the Queen*. She would still have the same duties, the same responsibilities, the same expectations.

And the anguish she saw on his face didn't make it any better.

"I don't like any of those options," he said, as if the words cost him. As if this all hurt him as much as it hurt her, and the funny thing was, she believed it did. Not that it changed anything. Not that anything could. But her foolish heart jolted all the same when he smiled again, just for her. "What if I had a better idea?"

CHAPTER SIX

MILA WASN'T SURE that it was a better idea at all.

In fact, she thought a few days later as she quit the palace for the September House, she was fairly certain that she had taken leave of her senses completely. And this time she did not have the excuse that she was off on a journey to experience a different sort of life, as prescribed by her own father.

This time she did not have any excuse at all.

Her mother fussed at her about everything and nothing, the way Alondra always did when one of her flock was leaving her—something Mila had to chant to herself to keep her smile welded to her face and the spirit of empathy in her heart.

"The kingdom has soldiered on through this very same crisis a number of times a year since antiquity," she reminded the Queen Mother.

Also my *mother*, she reminded herself, *who calls me only my title so she won't slip up and call me an endearment in front of government officials.*

"And we no longer have to send messengers by horse and cart. You can call me. If you must."

Alondra did not miss her daughter's faint emphasis on the word *must*.

By the time Mila sank into the back of the armored SUV that had been prepared for her, she was only too happy to sit back, close her eyes, and start counting the minutes of the drive that would take her to a month of something far closer to freedom than usual. That was as normal as her retreat itself. It wasn't that Mila didn't enjoy her life and her role. She did. But she also liked this tradition—the only version of a holiday a queen could have.

She was driven out of the city before the car started making its way around the lakes. One after the next. The car wove a path from lakeshore to rolling field to lake yet again, giving Mila a tour of the country itself.

It looked like a painting. It always had.

She supposed it was down to her to make certain it always would.

The car began to climb once more on the far side of the great valley. They took the steep switch-backed roads until the air grew colder and she could see that snow had already fallen on the highest peaks. Only then did they turn in through a set of unmarked but sturdy gates, then take a slightly less steep zigzag of a drive until they reached the house itself.

It had been built to be a kind of mirror of the palace that stood all the way down on the other end of the valley. It was too far to see with the naked eye, though she'd seen artists' renderings of the two buildings and the valley many times, as it was considered an iconic representation of Las Sosegadas. But the two royal dwellings couldn't have been more different.

Where the palace was a collection of spires and turrets, rising high above the kingdom's capital city like a beacon of prosperity and peace, the September House was more of a brooding affair. It had been built as a hunting cottage, but the word *cottage* didn't really apply. It had been expanded over the centuries so that now it was a cluster of different buildings that shouldn't have gone together at all.

Yet they always seemed to do so beautifully, to her eye.

Mila could feel the tension in her shoulders melt away as they pulled up and stopped before the stairs that led up to the heavy wooden doors.

The house was ready for her. All the lights were blazing against the bite of the cold this high up. She knew that the kitchen would be stocked full and that the staff who lived on the grounds would give her the space she liked. There would be deliveries of perishables twice a week and otherwise, unless she called them in, she would be left to her own devices.

Mila felt the lick of a familiar flame, deep within.

She let the driver carry her bags inside, because he would have been offended if she did not. And then she stood in the warm, welcoming hall that smelled the way it always did—of a hint of cinnamon and something citrusy—and waited until the car disappeared back down the long drive.

The flame within her danced higher.

The house had been built as a place to relax on a

grand scale. The library flowed into an atrium, then flowed out onto the terraces that were lovely in warmer weather, then seemed to roll off into the woods. She walked that way, but instead of heading outside she took the turn that would lead her into the rambling kitchen. Then to the old door that led down into the cellars.

The cellars housed some of the kingdom's finest wines, and many gifted bottles from abroad, but she walked past them. She kept on going down a long, cold corridor carved into the mountain, then down another flight of stairs that a scant few people even knew was there.

It had been hidden, deliberately. It was far off in the back and looked as if it should be little more than a closet. Mila pulled the keys from the pocket of her long skirt that she'd brought with her from the palace—another item she hid away in her private effects. She opened the door that looked like a forgotten closet and switched on the lone light that did little to beat back the shadows gathering there on the spiral stone stair. It looked and felt medieval, and her father had told her—when he'd told her about this family secret in the first place—that there were some arguments to be made that it might, in fact, date from that period.

But it had been put to great use in the last century's great wars.

Mila followed the cold stair down and around until she got to the heavy iron door at the bottom. She fit a second key into the lock there, and threw the dead bolt.

Then she pushed back the other bolts with her hands, and slowly, carefully, opened the heavy door.

And then smiled.

Because he was there, right where she'd told him to be.

Better yet, he was lounging against the wall of the tunnel that wound down for a mile or two and came out in an abandoned tomb in the nearby village. And even here, in the faint light from that single far-off bulb, Caius looked...

Perfect, Mila thought.

Rakish and beautiful and his gaze met hers, bright and hot, and warmed through with that particular spell work that was only his.

That same gleaming dragon deep within her stirred, and its tail seemed to snake through her, sending sensation spinning into every last cell.

"I feel like a spy," he told her, with that grin that suggested he quite liked that idea.

"You are now in possession of state secrets," she told him. "Use your power wisely."

"I think you know I always do."

And they were both smiling too much, Mila thought. She actually felt *giddy* and that could only be dangerous, because she couldn't pretend it was something to do with the pent-up air down here.

It was *her*. It was *him*.

It was the fact that he had suggested he join her here and she had immediately figured out how he could.

And here he was.

Giddy barely covered it.

Mila tried to cover up her reaction by motioning for him to come in. He did, with his usual nonchalance and nothing but a bag slung over one shoulder. She started fussing around with the bolts and the locks again, before she realized that all she'd done was leave them both crowded on top of each other.

At the bottom of a spiral stone stair.

With only the faintest little bit of light.

She cleared her throat. "The tunnels were built a very long time ago," she told him as if this was a tour of the September House that he had signed up for, the way tourists could do at the palace. "They have been used in any number of wars and minor skirmishes, as you can imagine. It is never a bad idea be difficult to find when people are calling for your head, or for a revolution, or are looking for simple and effective way to occupy a country."

"I always thought of the kingdom as somehow above the whims of war or invading armies," Caius said.

"We would like to be," she replied. "The tunnels help. So do the mountains."

And she was afraid, suddenly, that he would be able to hear her heart pounding in her chest if she stayed still any longer. Mila turned abruptly, as if she had never had a lesson in comportment in her life, headed back up the stairs. *Sprinted* back the stairs, more like.

She cautioned herself to slow down, but she felt as if she was some kind of mythological creature, granted a wish. All she had to do was lead Caius up from the underworld.

Mila wanted to glance back, but she didn't dare. Everyone knew what happened if she did.

Back in the main part of the house, she found herself buffeted by the strangest feelings. And it took her some while to realize that she felt...out of place. As if she didn't quite know what to do with herself.

The moment she identified that sensation, she very nearly laughed. Because she couldn't recall feeling like that in a long, long time.

And the last time she had, she had been setting out on the adventure that would lead her to him.

"Well," she said, all formal and stiff after she'd led him on a small sort of tour. And felt as if her skin was seven sizes too small on her body while *he* seemed only to become more boneless with every step. "I don't know what your intention was when you suggested this—"

"Yes, you did," Caius replied.

They had made it to the low-slung, relaxed living area, all soft, aged leather and a fireplace stocked with wood, ready to light.

He tossed his bag on one of the sofas, and then turned toward her with a look of intent.

And everything in her flashed into a white-hot coil of need. Desire.

That dragon testing its gleam, stretching out inside her.

"We can't possibly just *leap*—" she began, almost desperately, though she didn't step away. She didn't move a single inch.

"We can." He stopped before her, his bright eyes

alight. "Take the leap, Mila. Let's see if we can find our wings again."

Then Caius simply pulled her into his arms, lifting her high above him so he could slide her back down the length of his body.

Mila's mind went blank with delight, though it seemed as if her mouth still wanted to form words. As if there was an argument waiting, there on her tongue.

But her body knew exactly what to do.

She wrapped herself around him as he slid her down the length of his torso. And so by the time he settled her, his hands gripping her bottom and her legs around his hips, she could no longer tell who was kissing who.

It felt too good. It was a *catastrophe*.

A cataclysmic eruption of everything she had put on hold, everything she had tried to forget, everything that had always been there, waiting.

And this was no kiss stolen on the balcony where anyone might happen along.

Mila knew that both of them were fully aware that no one was going to interrupt them here.

That for the first time since she'd looked up and seen that he'd walked back into her life with that same smile on his face, they were well and truly on their own.

And this was what that meant. What that had always meant.

That blazing fire. The dragon's mighty roar.

And the sheer, impossible joy of it.

She dug her hands into his hair and found herself rocking against him, to make it better. To make it worse.

And also because she couldn't stop.

He didn't wait another moment. Caius toppled them both down onto the nearest couch, and then everything seemed to implode even more.

One implosion after the next, as if they might die like this, wrapped up in each other—and Mila wasn't sure she'd mind.

He pressed her down into the embrace of the sofa, and she *bloomed* beneath him. Had she worn this particular airy skirt in the hopes that it would go this way? Had she known that it would be like this—that his hands would be on her thighs, smoothing their way up to the V where her thighs met, so he could stroke his way into her softness while his tongue did the same dance with hers?

Maybe she'd only dreamed it, for years, but now it was real.

Neither one of them spoke. Because this was the same wildfire that had always consumed them, only this time, it was...*more*.

More intense. More demanding.

More dangerous, Mila managed to think, but that didn't stop her.

Her hands were beneath his shirt, finding their way to those muscles of his. She was alternately clinging onto him or digging into him, depending on what he was doing with first one long finger, then two.

And the thing about Caius is that he knew exactly what he was doing.

He threw her over the cliff too easily and she found her wings there, laughing as she shook and shattered.

That he moved over her, reaching down between them to free himself, before thrusting his way home.

For a moment, then, there was only *this*.

The sheer, impossible glory of it.

He filled her completely. It had been so long.

They were locked together, their gazes, their bodies. It was as if there was no telling where one of them ended and the other began.

She clenched around him, unable to stop herself, and felt him as he shivered in response.

And then that shiver seemed to roll through her, so that suddenly she was shattering apart all over again, but he stayed where he was, hot and hard and still so deep inside of her.

She slid her hands around the front of his chest, still tucked there under his shirt, and for a long, long while, there was only shaking apart. Shaking back to life.

Shaking and shaking and shaking.

When she opened her eyes again his magical gaze, like nothing short of spell work, was all she could see.

"I want to see you." She swallowed, hard. "I'm still protected. But I want to *see* you, Caius."

She had never been more grateful that she had taken her sister's advice and gone on birth control when they were still teenagers.

I don't... Mila had blushed. *I mean, I haven't...*

It isn't about what you're doing or not doing, Carliz had said. *It's about setting a precedent so that no one but you ever knows if you need it or not.*

Mila made a mental note to send her sister a gift.

Caius blew out a breath. He rested his forehead against hers, holding himself there for one breath. Another.

Then he withdrew, and that felt like grief all over again. It rolled through her too much like a sob.

But he was only shrugging out of his shirt. He wore some kind of chain around his neck but he pulled that off too, crossing over to his bag and tossing it all there, followed by the rest of his clothes. Mila followed suit, and he crossed back to her he made a very low, very male sound of appreciation that she was naked, too.

Then he rolled her with him as he lay back down, so that she ended up between the back of the sofa and the glorious wall of his body.

She thought he would say something then. But there was no curve in the corner of his mouth. His eyes were like magic, and they were all she could see, still.

And suddenly everything felt sacred.

Caius smoothed a hand over her face, this thumb moving over her lips. Then he pulled her over the length of his body as he turned on his back, settling her astride him.

And then, with his hands at her hips to encourage her, to command her, they both seemed to hold their breath at the same time she braced herself against his torso and angled her body to take the full, thick length of him deep inside her once again.

"*My* Majesty," he growled.

Then Mila tipped back her head, arched her back, and lost herself in the rhythm he had taught her five years ago.

It was the same dance, but it felt like new.

They were the same people, but five years' difference had changed everything. And nothing. And somewhere in the tension between those two things, there was *this*.

The way she rocked against him, half blind with need and pleasure and spinning out on the sheer beauty of the heat they made together. On her softness and his hardness. On all the ways they fit so well, so perfectly.

Just like five years ago, he met her as she moved, until the dragon was in flight and everything was fire.

"You had better hurry, my queen," he told her as the fires built. "You're running out of time."

Mila laughed at that, throwing back the hair he'd taken down with his greedy hands. She moved faster, wilder. And then, finding his gaze and holding it, she reached down between them and found the center of her own need.

And she hurtled herself toward that edge.

But he was there with her as she leaped—

And then it was nothing but a soaring, sweet flight with fireworks all around, comets and shooting stars.

Until she floated back down to earth and caught herself right where she wanted to be, with her face tucked into the crook of his neck.

Just like coming home, she thought.

Or maybe she said it out loud, because there was an echoing rumble in his chest.

But there was no point worrying about that now.

She drifted off to sleep, in a way she knew she hadn't done since Noemí had walked into that room in California and curtseyed to the new queen. She slept the way a monarch never could, because she knew that with his arms around her, he would protect her from whatever came. That she could trust him to take care of her.

And as she drifted there, half awake and half asleep, she knew too well how dangerous it was to think these things. How they had led her to marry him in the first place, which was the cause of all this trouble.

But it didn't feel like trouble today.

It felt like lifetimes later when she stirred and found that he had disentangled them, but still lay there with her, his gaze on the ceiling. She took stock, finding tiny little remnants of sensation like undercurrents, running beneath her skin. There was the endless list of things she ought to have been worried about—but this was the September House. Unless and until there was a pressing matter of state to deal with, she did not have to worry about anything.

That was the whole point.

So she propped up her chin on her hands and looked at him, at those impossibly artistic lines of his beautiful face.

"So," she said.

She could feel laughter move in him though the only sign of it on his face was the shift in his gaze, that dark amber lightning. "So," he agreed.

There were too many things she wanted to ask him. But all of them were huge. Weighty and impossible when she had the feeling that this thing between them, just now, was like spun glass. It would be easy enough to hurl it to the floor and watch it shatter into shards too small to ever put back together. Too easy.

Alternatively, she could go the other way and blow the glass into shapes and colors, just to see. Just to make something different.

Or possibly because you can't face the truth, a voice inside her scolded.

But she accepted that.

"Where did you go?" Mila asked instead. "After California?"

It was a risky proposition. She knew that before he slid a gaze her way, one brow lifted. As if to ask, *Do you really dare?*

But she gazed right back at him, steadily.

And he could have been the one to take that little bit of glass and throw it against the wall, but he didn't. "I needed a project," he said. "Something to lose myself in."

She did him the courtesy of not asking what he meant. Because looking back, she supposed that that's what she'd had, too. The project of becoming *the Queen.* Of morning her father. Of planning her coronation. Of turning herself into the sovereign.

There had been no time to think about what might have been.

Or perhaps it was more accurate to say that every time she had thought about it, she had chastised herself for losing focus.

And despite all of those other things to focus on, it had still been so hard she was sometimes surprised she'd survived it. Though she didn't like to think about that.

"I started a production company," he said, with a self-deprecating sort of laugh. She remembered him sitting in the firelight on that long hike, talking about his childhood and how his parents had never been there for him, but that there had always been the cinema. There had always been movies to watch and characters to depend on instead. "Such companies are thick on the ground in Hollywood and most of them fail. Usually because of the enormous ego of the person whose vanity is funding the project in the first place. I could easily have taken that route, with my rather robust ego. But I chose instead to have an ego about the projects, not me."

"That is the only way," Mila agreed. "Vanity is a mirror. True confidence is a path forward."

"Indeed." She had forgotten the way he liked to run his fingers through her hair, letting the silken strands dance over his palm. "The company still exists. We are small, but so far, have a not-unimpressive track record." Another self-deprecating sound. "It is something to do."

It would have been easy to laugh at that, and the way he said it encouraged that, clearly.

But Mila didn't. She studied him instead. "You're proud of what you've done. You should be. It's not a small thing when you make a dream come true, Caius."

His expression was wry. "It is not a big thing either, not when one is encumbered with a portfolio like mine."

"Don't worry," she said, smiling at him. "I won't tell anyone that secretly, deep down, the famously jaded Caius Candriano cares deeply about the things he makes."

And she was surprised, then, when he shifted, moving to sit up. And she had a moment of something like dizziness that they were sitting there, disheveled and undressed, and she didn't have to worry about how it would look should someone stumble in.

About what she would do or how she would explain this away.

Something seemed to clutch at her, but she didn't know what it was. She pushed it aside, because Caius had his elbows on his knees and was shoving his hair back from his brow with both hands.

"This is the part I try to forget," he said in a low voice. "I don't want you to understand me, Mila. Not when that understanding doesn't go anywhere. Not when it's like throwing stones at the moon."

She sighed, and that clutching thing inside her intensified. "Do we have to do this now?"

But he didn't answer her. He raked a hand through his hair instead, and the laugh he let out twisted in her, too sharp. Too hard.

"I made the films for you." When she didn't respond to that, or not with words, anyway, he turned so he could look at her. "You must know that, surely. I made them all for you. Love stories, writ large. Like love letters I did not dare send to your palace."

He gazed at her. And she shook her head, slowly.

Then again. "I didn't know," she told him. When he looked incredulous, she lifted her hands. "I do not watch as many television shows or films as other peo-

ple do. I hate to stumble over some or other representation of myself, or royalty in general. I prefer books."

And for a moment, she thought he might explode.
She'd seen his temper before—always a bright flare
followed by instant regret. As if he bubbled over sometimes, could not contain it, and then wished that he had.

But then, she thought the next moment, that was a
different version of him.

This version looked at her with a sad curve of that
sensual mouth of his and a kind of bleakness in his
gaze. "That sounds about right. I am nothing if not pre-
dictable. Forever tilting at windmills when you have
no use for wind, or mills, or down-market knights of
any kind."

She moved closer to him so she could take his face
in her hands. She pressed her lips to that space between
his brows. To one eyelid, then the next. She pressed
kisses everywhere her lips could touch, from temple
to chin to that corner of his mouth where that mocking little curve lived. She kissed him over and over,
until she felt the tension in his big, rangy body ease.

And when she pulled back, there was something
sweet there between them. Something new.

"What I can give you," she told him quietly, sol-
emnly, "is September. Will you take it?"

And she knew he would. They were twined together
again, tangled up tight. She knew he wasn't going to
storm back out of those tunnels. Not today.

Because they were nothing if not trapped here together.

Maybe she wanted him to admit to it.

"I will take it," he said, as if they were making vows again. "But Mila, I warn you, that will not be the only thing I take."

And she chose, then, to misunderstand him. She made her smile go sultry. And then she licked at his mouth, kissing him deep.

Chasing that dragon once again.

"Challenge accepted," she whispered, and then she wrapped herself around him once more, and set them both into flight.

CHAPTER SEVEN

SEPTEMBER WAS LIKE a dream—the kind of dream that Caius had woken up from, wild with desire, unsettled, and without her, more times than he could count over these past five years.

This high in the mountains, autumn was already making its appearance. The mornings were cold, though they warmed into achingly blue days and crisp nights that came earlier all the time. The trees were turning bright, bold colors, as if gripping on tight to the long summer days already past. Caius could relate.

It was a dream, these September days, but Caius could not fool himself the way he had once before. Because this time, he knew how this dream was going to end. There was no point in imagining otherwise, the way he had once before.

What he couldn't understand was how, knowing what was to come, he still couldn't bring himself to change a thing.

"I thought you were going to enact some kind of dastardly revenge plan," Mila said one evening as they moved around the kitchen together. They had taken to playing music as they assembled their meals, the kitchen brightly lit against the dark that waited there outside the windows, music dancing in the air like some kind of spell to keep the world away.

The kind of spell Caius had wished he'd known as a child, forever languishing in hotel rooms and dreaming of exactly this kind of life. Of becoming the kind of person who was capable of this kind of life. This ease and sweetness instead of his mother's chaotic rages. This pervasive wave of something he thought might be happiness, instead of the battle to assess his mother's condition in any moment and figure out how to pretend to be whatever version of her son she might have decided he was that hour.

It was easy, here, to pretend they were other people. People who did not play vicious games with one another and call it *family*. People who did not fight nasty little wars for supremacy, imagining that somehow they might escape the Countess's notice—that too-sharp focus that always boded ill.

Here in the September House, they did none of those things.

Here they were different people entirely. People who prepared food because it was good and put out table settings because they were pretty, and then enjoyed each other's company when they sat down. People who talked of the weather, not because they had nothing else to say, but because even the most innocuous conversations were layered and textured with all the ways they took each other apart and put each other back together when they were naked.

As if it was all the same thing, in one form or another.

Mila did not cook in the classic sense. But she was a deft hand at putting together ingredients that were preprepared for her. He discovered that she was a big fan of a hearty soup or a stew, accompanied by freshly baked bread with a liberal application of butter. That she would eat it night and day, if possible.

Caius contributed his own skills, which were not in-considerable—because he had developed a deep loath-ing of delivered food when he was young, so had taught himself to cook—to add a bit of variety to the menu.

And this was how they sank in deep to this long September dream of the kind of domestic bliss neither one of them was likely to have, and certainly not with each other. They prepared all their meals together and ate them slowly while having wide-ranging conversa-tions on every topic under the sun. They fought, not always amicably, over the books they'd both read. They avoided the news and laughed at each other's stories. They took long walks around the property, taking in the mountain air. They even did a bit of hiking the way they had all those years ago.

And they feasted on each other, at every opportu-nity, as if they could never get enough.

Because, he supposed, they both knew the inevi-table end was coming. They both knew there was no future. Caius had to make sure that every moment of this month was memorable enough to last them both a lifetime.

He took that calling very, very seriously.

And so they indulged themselves in every scrap of sensuality they could find. The stately old hunting lodge offered an endless array of places to explore. From the hot springs that some enterprising member of the royal family had erected an entire bathhouse around in centuries past to a wide selection of beds and showers, including his favorite of those—the outdoor shower that let the stars shine in.

Yet she wanted to know if, through all of this, this banquet of the senses in all its forms, he was plotting revenge.

"You really do have a dim view of me, don't you," he said.

She was stirring the night's big meal, a crock of lamb stew that filled the kitchen with its rich scent. She turned, looking around at him in surprise, the steam from the simmering pot making her cheeks red.

And Mila was always beautiful. There was no denying that. Queen Mila was a study in contemporary elegance. Every outfit he'd seen her photographed in reached new heights of sophistication, as if she challenged herself daily to redefine chic for the modern world.

But her ability to casually, offhandedly achieve the same result without a cadre of attendants amazed him daily. She was a wonder. Today she was wearing her hair in two braids, each one wound into its own bun on the back of her head. He had watched her fix them that way herself. She was still wearing the sleek leggings she'd worn out on their walk, with colorful knit socks pulled halfway up her shins. And an oversized sweater in a fine, lush wool that managed to make all of that look not like a lumberjack or even all that casual, but like royalty.

He acknowledged the possibility that this was just… her.

"A dim view of you?" she repeated. She shook her head as if he wasn't making sense. "I…don't?"

"You do." Caius had been slicing one of the fresh baguettes that turned up at the kitchen door like clockwork and needed only to be baked through. He set the knife down, then propped himself up on his hands against the great butcher block on the island in the center of the sprawling kitchen. "You do, Mila. That's not an indictment. I've spent my entire life making certain that I'm underestimated at every turn. I can't get angry when my efforts are successful, can I?"

She studied him with those solemn, clever gray eyes. "Yet you seem angry."

"What I am," he said, and it was a challenge to keep his voice calm when he knew it should not have been, "is viewing everything that happened between us with new eyes."

They had danced around this topic since he'd gotten here, after trekking miles through underground, clearly little-used tunnels, hoping that she hadn't sent him off to march his way into the dungeons she'd mentioned. But this was different. She didn't cross her arms. She didn't straighten her shoulders and tip her head in that regal way of hers—to let him know *the Queen* was in the room.

She only waited, studying him, as if she didn't know what he was going to say.

It was strange how cheering that notion was.

But he didn't speak. And the silence stretched out between them. Eventually, she swallowed. "Are you going to say something?"

"There is nothing to say." He shrugged. "I have said it."

"How ominous," Mila murmured.

Caius pushed back from the butcher block and returned his attention to the bread. "My mother is getting married."

He sensed Mila's confusion at that change of subject but when he glanced at her, she had already turned back to the stew bubbling on the range, stirring it again. "I don't know whether to offer you congratulations or condolences."

"She wants me to attend, of course. My sister—"

"Lavinia," Mila said, warmly enough that it made something in him squeeze tight.

He nodded. "She keeps calling to tell me how important it is to the Countess that I be there. How devastated she will be if I don't turn up."

"Will you go?"

Caius set the knife down on the cutting board. "It's not that my mother wants my emotional support or has tender feelings about gathering the family together. That's not her style. I'm not entirely certain she's capable of tender feelings. She wants my presence to raise her profile. She wants to make sure that the paparazzi, who must be as tired of tracking her marital status as anyone else, will be there to cover it. Because nothing makes my mother feel alive like seeing herself in newspapers."

"I thought that's what you liked." Mila glanced back over her shoulder at him, and there was nothing accusing in her expression. If anything, she looked...concerned. For him. He didn't like how that sat heavy on him, then pressed down hard. "You used to talk extensively about what it was like to be seen as a kind of conduit for people." She put the big wooden spoon to the side of the pot, and then drifted over from the range so that she faced him directly across the center island. "To be perfectly honest, I think I drew on that quite a bit in my first days as queen. You once told me that the most important skill you'd ever mastered was being the kind of mirror that anyone who looked into believed was bespoke." She shrugged, giving him a small smile. "See? I've never forgotten it."

He was stunned by that. If she had picked up that pot simmering away behind her and whacked him with it, he could not have been more stunned—but there was an urgency in him, now. There was something winding its way through him, past the heaviness of her concern for him and the conclusive proof she'd just given him now, that she had not forgotten him. That she had held on to things he'd told her.

That it had mattered, those stolen weeks in California too long ago now to bear.

There were a great many reasons to keep his counsel in this moment, Caius knew, but he didn't. He couldn't.

"I have never been more surprised in my life," he said quietly, "then when I learned that what I considered my superpower—the ability to read any room I went into—was a product of being raised by the kind of terrible people who would, years later, hound the child they'd neglected for clout." But he didn't want to talk about his mother. He was studying Mila's face. "I've never asked you how hard it was. It must have been nothing short of terrible for you, to have no time to prepare."

He remembered that day in the sort of detail he would have thought usually reserved for, say, terrible accidents. He'd walked into the shower a married man, not unaware of the challenges ahead of them due to their different stations, but secure in what they were to and for each other.

He'd walked out to meet the Queen.

"You prepare for the ceremony," she told him in a hushed voice. "For the steps that you'll take and the way that you'll present yourself. You don't do it alone. My father planned it with me. His team and mine talked all the time about the plans. Always the plans. Always making it sound like a great festival of some kind." She gave him a wry little smile, then, that broke his heart. "But you never talk about how much it hurts."

One of her hands drifted to her chest, directly over her heart, in a gesture that he knew, somehow, was unconscious. It made his own heart ache even more.

"It would be unseemly to talk about how it feels. And so you rely on all of that planning, and all of the pomp and circumstance. You're busy thinking about how it looks, and what message you're sending, and how the people are perceiving you… And it turns out that it's a crutch." Mila looked almost lost, for a moment, but then her gray gaze found his again. So at least he could be lost with her. "It's much easier to think about how to become a queen than it is to mourn the death of your father. To be honest with you, I'm not sure I ever have."

"And one day, if you do your duty, your child will have to do the same thing."

He realized after he said it how she could take that. How she might see it as a jab, but she didn't. If anything, her smile grew deeper.

More wry, if that was possible. "I don't think that's the privilege of royalty. I am fairly sure that's just life. We will all of us mourn our parents, if we are lucky."

"You consider that lucky?"

"The alternative is that they would have to mourn us," she said quietly.

"Mila." He said her name so urgently. There could be no mistaking that. He saw the way her eyes widened. But then again, if he wasn't mistaken, she was holding her breath. "Mila, why did you leave me?"

"You know the answer to that. We are discussing the answer to that right now."

"That's not what I mean. You know it's not."

He thought she would default to an instant denial, but she didn't. Instead, she looked away for a moment, out toward the windows, where the night was already dark and seemed to press against the glass. She looked…softer than usual.

Caius realized that it was surprising to think of her as fragile. He never had. She was so good at exuding all that regal energy. She was so good at making it seem as if she was far too iconic to be human at all.

He was going to have to think about the fact he'd let himself believe that, when he knew better.

"Putting aside all the many heart attacks the palace would have over your presence in the tabloids," Mila began.

"Because the tabloids are bastions of truth, of course. Everyone knows that."

He couldn't seem to help himself.

Mila only held his gaze. "Whether the stories are true or not isn't the issue. The issue is the regularity of your appearances and the kinds of places and people you have frequented over the years." Her eyes were so gray. So grave. "This isn't a lecture. It's an explanation. But that's an excuse, I think."

"You think."

"It's *this*," she said, and waved a hand back and forth between them.

He thought of the way that same hand had wrapped around the hardest part of him earlier in the shower, las she'd looked up at him so boldly while taking him into her mouth.

"This…intensity. How does that fit into my life? Or your life, for that matter?"

She could hardly *think* around the man. Much less *rule* in the way that was required of her. Or she couldn't imagine how she might go about it, anyway. It felt impossible.

"Do you know what I often wonder?" But she didn't wait for him to answer that. "If I hadn't left you, you almost certainly would have left me. If I had to guess, I would say that you would have found a way to manufacture some scandal or another so that I would have no choice but to leave."

"Again." His voice was a mere scratch. "It really is a dim view, isn't it?"

He could see she didn't like that by the way her chin inched up. "It's who you are. It's who *I* am. Those things can't mesh."

"You mean your pedigreed status and the fact I am a mongrel, I suppose."

"I mean that you like to immerse yourself in intensity. You like projects with a beginning and an end, and when it's done, you move on. And I..." She sighed, and shook her head a little as if the sigh was a cold wind and now she could not shake the chill. "Everything I do must be sealed in eternity. I must be a walking, talking study in permanence. How could it ever work?"

"It does work, Mila. Behold, it's working right now."

"We are magic," she agreed, though her voice was rougher than he'd heard it in years. Since she had looked at him with the same gray eyes but a stranger's face and had said, *There has been some news. My father, the King, is dead.* Here, now, she leaned a little bit closer over that island between them. "But it can only be a temporary magic, Caius. Like before. I thought you understood."

But she laughed—looking startled—when he came around the island, swept her into his arms, and then demonstrated how powerful his *temporary magic* was, right there on the old wood table.

More than once, for good measure.

Still, Caius found he continued to brood over that a day or two later.

She'd had to take an extra call that day, in the alcove off the main living room that she'd told him at least five of her predecessors had sat in to do the work of the kingdom. He stayed nearer the fire, but he could hear the cool, collected way she spoke to her ministers. Not the words themselves, but her cadence. Her tone.

It didn't matter what she was saying. It was all regal.

Every single thing that made Mila who she was, he understood, was another nail in the coffin that was the two of them. And this month that was winnowing its way out.

He pulled out his mobile and didn't bother scrolling through his messages. He knew what he would see— that his voicemail was full and there were so many texts that he might as well toss the bloody thing off the side of the mountain, then start over.

The way he did several times a year, usually without explanation. Everyone he wanted to talk to always found him again.

But he didn't get rid of his mobile just yet, though the mountainside beckoned. Instead, he looked up a number he rarely called, then pressed the call button before he could think better of it.

Well. Not *before* he thought better. Just before *think better of it* could stop him.

It rang and rang. And when it was finally answered, it was in a great flurry that shouted *drama is occurring and you might be the cause* and he could feel himself tensing already. Before she even said a word.

Though it was always the same word. Lavinia and he had long ago decided that she could not recall their names. Not in a pinch.

"*Darling.* I was beginning to think the worst."

"Hello, Countess," Caius drawled. Because his mother did not take kindly to the term *mother.* Or any other version of that word. Or anything that suggested an age differential of any kind.

The last time he'd tried he had been six. He had gone racing into her room, called her Mama, and had gotten slapped soundly across the face.

After all, she'd been entertaining. It had been his fault.

She had made certain he knew that he'd done it to himself.

Now, his mother was prattling on, the way she did. It was always so tempting to think of her as insubstantial when she wittered on about dresses and wherever she was living now and the cost of something after which he hadn't inquired.

But Caius knew that she was a shark and this was how she circled, looking for blood.

"I will come to your wedding," he said abruptly, cutting her off. "But only on the condition that nobody knows I'm there."

His mother laughed in obvious incomprehension, and there was nothing about that sound that anyone would describe as *insubstantial.* "I have no earthly idea what that means."

"It's very simple." He sat back in the old, soft leather couch and stared up at the art on the wall before him, a finely rendered landscape painting. Likely of a view from this house. "I will attend to support you, as your son. But I don't want the papers to catch wind of it."

"Darling, the papers don't *catch wind* of anything." Now she sounded like the shark she was, teeth and all. "They follow you around. Surely you know this."

"Sometimes they follow me around, and sometimes people call them to let them know where I'll be," Caius countered. "I'm going to need you to promise me that won't happen this time."

"Caius." When it mattered, apparently, his mother did actually know his name. "This is all very childish. You are a public figure, like it or not. And there's a certain expectation when it comes to our family. The people have come to require certain things of us. It's the least we can do to give them that."

But he was sitting in the September House, in the company of a queen. An actual queen who lived her life for her people. Who had walked away from him for them. Who would do it again.

A woman who did these things for duty, not fame.

"You have my permission, indeed, my encouragement, to seek out that attention all on your own," he told his mother. "With my compliments."

"Don't you dare do this," his mother seethed at him, and he thought, *There she is*. It was that instant flip from one face to another that he remembered so well, and he could hear it in her voice. He didn't have to have eyes on her because he knew exactly what it looked like. One moment, his beautiful mother, all that was lovely and graceful. The next, the monster who wore that shining vision as a costume and was never too far from the surface. "After all I've done for you."

"And what was that again?" Caius asked, making sure he sounded bored.

He wasn't. Because he supposed there was still that little six-year-old inside him somewhere, wishing he'd had that *mama* he'd gone looking for. But if the Countess ever got wind of the possibility he might have actual feelings, she would hunt him down and try to eat him alive. That was her favorite pastime.

Caius knew her well enough to know that for a certainty.

But maybe, as he sat in this royal hunting lodge as the Queen's guilty secret, he was starting to wonder who *he* was.

"I was in labor for seventy-two thankless hours," his mother railed at him. He thought she was slipping, or confusing him with his half siblings. Usually she said ninety hours, for the drama. "And raising you was no walk in the park, Caius. Your father was a horrid monster. You can't imagine the things I suffered!"

"Surely if that's true, you would have seen it before the wedding and shouldn't have married him," Caius drawled, because he had not let her wind him up in a long, long time.

Maybe his father was a monster, too. He had always seemed deeply sad and ineffective to Caius, but then, people were different with their intimate partners. But there was nothing he could do about a marriage she'd left when Caius was small. None of the things she claimed she'd suffered excused her.

And he couldn't help but notice that she only used her excuses to land what she hoped were mortal blows.

"And this is what I get," the Countess snarled, switching tacks yet again. "As if it is such a hardship to do the only thing you've ever been any good at. Simply show up. Smile. Practice that empty charm of yours that you throw around like confetti." And she laughed as if she could see him. As if he'd let his guard fall when he knew he hadn't. She was good at that, too. "That's all you've ever had to do, Caius. No one *wants* anything from you. No one *expects* anything from you. You drift through your life as meaningless as the day you were born. All that's needed from you—ever—is that you stand still long enough for the right pictures to be taken. How can that possibly be a trial? Even for you?"

He didn't mean to hang up on her. Or he didn't think he did.

But he found himself staring at the mobile in his hand, the call ended, and a selection of some very unflattering thoughts taking space in his brain.

She'd like that, he knew. She'd like to think she'd gotten to him.

If I could slap you again, she'd said at one of her weddings, *I would do it harder, so it taught you something.*

In case he'd been tempted to believe that she might harbor regrets. Or have amnesia about her own behavior.

In case he took his sister's position and tried thinking of her as a flawed human who had used what few, poor tools she had—instead of the shark she had always been and always would be.

Caius could still hear *the Queen* from the other room. Cool. Commanding. When this was the same woman who had sobbed in his arms only an hour ago, digging her fingernails into his back and leaving her trademark trail of half-moon crescents down the length of his spine.

One of these times, she had said later, sprawled out beside him and panting wildly, *you will break me down into too many pieces. They'll never put me back together again.*

But then, at the appointed time, she had risen from the bed without question or any excuses. She had pulled herself together in a flash, requiring no one's help to put her own pieces back, right where they belonged.

Something deep inside of him seemed to tremble at that, as if the ground beneath his feet was giving way.

He punched the button again to ring his sister.

"She's already on the other line," Lavinia said crossly, in lieu of any greeting. "What did you expect would happen, having a go at her like that? I'm not sure I'll ever talk her down."

"Then don't," Caius replied shortly.

His sister was quiet. He heard her mutter something, as if excusing herself, and then the sounds around her changed. He heard a door shut and imagined her walking from one room to the next, leaving whatever social situation she was in. Taking his call the way he would if taking her call in similar situations. A roll of the eye. A few choice words, mouthed to her friends.

All of these performances.

"I have a novel idea," he said into her ear. "What if you don't try to talk her down? What if we ignore her?"

"I didn't realize that was an option available to us," Lavinia said dryly. "Ignoring her and hoping she'd go away never bore any fruit that I can recall."

"All I did was tell her that I didn't want my picture in the paper if I went to her wedding," Caius said.

His sister sighed. "Why on earth would you tell her that?"

"Because I don't want my picture used as currency to buy things I don't value," he bit out, and there was a different sort of silence then.

And he knew why. He hadn't laughed. He hadn't sounded lazy, or amused, or deeply jaded.

If anything, he had sounded stern and *that* was something he never did. Not with Lavinia. Not with anyone, really. Not even with himself, if he could avoid it.

"Are you…?" He heard Lavinia blow out a breath. "Are you all right, Caius?"

"I would like to see what my life looks like if it is not a performance," Caius told her, the words welling up from within as if he had prepared them. Or as if they had been trying to come out for a long, long time. "If I am not the poster boy for the bad behavior of every single person I am related to, through no fault of my own. It occurred to me to wonder what it must be like not to have pictures of myself staring back at me from every newsstand, no matter where I go."

"You've done this before. The last time, you wandered off into the wilderness, as I recall. Did you learn something then? Because my memory is that you wandered back out of the mountains and became a tabloid darling all over again, overnight."

His sister sounded exasperated, but Caius looked up. Maybe he'd sensed something. Maybe she'd made a faint noise.

But either way, Mila was there. She was standing in the doorway, watching him.

And her face was caught somewhere between the Mila he had been with all these weeks and the Queen. He wanted to ask her which one was real, but she wasn't like him. She hadn't created her role in response to a mother like the Countess. She had been born to be the Queen.

She was both Mila *and* the Queen.

He'd gotten that wrong, last time.

Because last time he'd been so sure that he knew himself that well, too. He'd been wrong about a lot of things.

"I will tell you what I learned," he said into his mobile, his eyes on Mila. "Wandering around this planet with only my own two feet to guide me from one place to another made it clear that I have more to offer than a photo op. The Countess is under the impression that all I have to bring to the table is a smile. In which case, I suggest she find a cardboard cutout of me. She can use that at her wedding, with my compliments. Because what I learned all of those years ago, hiking around in places where nobody recognized me at all, was that anonymity is a gift."

"Oh, Caius," Lavinia said, laughing now. "You only think that because it was a choice. You've never seen a stage you didn't climb up on, then position yourself dead center. Why pretend otherwise?"

"Lavinia," he said, almost gently. "I'm not going to her wedding. Or any future weddings. Ever."

Then he hung up on her, too.

"That seemed intense," Mila said after a moment, when all they did was look at each other across the expanse of the long room. "Families always are, I know."

He wanted to tell her all the things that were swirling around inside of him, all of the odd thoughts and new understandings that he wasn't sure he really wanted. He wanted to tell her that he wasn't temporary, that he didn't *want* to be temporary.

That just because he was good at center stage didn't mean he liked it.

"Do you know why I like producing?" he asked instead. And he must have looked as rough as he felt, because all she did was shake her head, *no*.

And the tiniest little frown appeared between her eyes.

"I like fitting the pieces together," he said, and he knew he was losing it because he sounded so vehement about it. Not the faintest hint of an incoming joke or any small drop of self-deprecation. But he couldn't seem to stop. "I like putting the right people into the correct rooms. Making sure the trains run on time. That everyone is paid. That everything works the way it's meant to work. When most people see a beautiful sports car, they *ooh* and *ahh* over the shape of it. The form. How it looks when it drives. But what fascinates me is what's under the hood. That's what I like."

He stopped himself from saying, *That's who I am*.

For a moment, they held each other's gaze.

But then, Mila laughed.

And he didn't know how to tell her that the sound splashed over him like acid. "You have always been a great many things, Caius. But I would never consider you a *mechanic*."

He should have told her then. He could have. He could have dug down into that trembling place inside, where everything was unsteady and new, glaring and terrible. He could have torn herself open, and *showed* her who he was.

That it was no laughing matter—

But his mother's voice was in his head, snide and harsh, telling him exactly what he was good at.

So all he did was smile when she came closer, and laugh along with her, careful to make sure he was charming. So goddamned charming, because that was the only thing anyone ever saw when they looked at him.

Even Mila, apparently. After everything.

CHAPTER EIGHT

MILA KNEW THAT something had changed after that day she'd heard him on a call she wasn't sure he'd meant her to witness. Something was different, though she couldn't put her finger on it.

She wasn't sure she liked that *yearning* thing inside her that wanted to know him inside and out in ways she certainly didn't want to be known herself. She wasn't sure she liked any of the messy, impossible things she felt these days, come to that.

Then again, September was waning all around them no matter how they filled their stolen days. It felt to her as if both she and Caius were on edge.

It was there in the way they devoured each other, but talked less. Everything was heat and flame, until she began to wonder if they would both burn to a crisp up here on her month away. The kingdom would look up and see nothing but a bright and burning torch where the September House had been.

Some part of her, she was unnerved to discover, actually craved that. As if self-immolation was that perfect solution she still hadn't been able to find. Instead of a daydream of pure, outrageous selfishness.

Not to mention anathema to everything she'd always believed she was.

But that was the trouble with spending time with Caius. She began to imagine that almost anything was possible.

When she knew better.

No matter how she agonized, no matter all the what-ifs that sometimes kept her awake at night wrapped up in his arms—thinking through one implausible scenario after the next—she knew better.

Her life had been planned from the start. It had never been her own, no matter those stolen weeks with him. It wasn't hers to give away to her *feelings*—something she'd seemed to understand more fully the last time.

Yet the more torn-up she felt that their end was nearing, the more ravenous he became.

And though she prided herself on never shying away from a difficult conversation, that, too, was different when it was Caius. She tried to tell herself that was only because they had both known, this time, that there would be nothing else.

Maybe this was simply how it would be between them this time, in lieu of any unpleasant scenes.

She told herself she ought to be happy with that. But what she felt, instead, was that she'd miscalculated. There would be no grand ceremonies to throw herself into on the other side of him this time. She had nowhere to ascend now that she was already Queen. She did not have to race home to the palace to comfort her sister, who had never enjoyed as peaceful a relationship with their father as she had. Or to perform her duties seamlessly and beautifully for her mother, who would not speak of her grief, only the future that Mila needed to embody to make it all right that her husband, the King, was gone.

It was beginning to seem clear that she might find this parting more difficult to bear than the last, and with less distraction. Fewer great griefs.

There would be no state funerals or coronations to concern herself with once September ended. There would only be whatever was left of her heart in his wake.

"Where will you go next?" she asked him on one of their last nights in the house, though neither one of them had mentioned *next*.

Until now, she supposed. Obliquely.

They'd thrown together one of their typical dinners tonight and she was trying her best not to let herself get too emotional—something she had never had to worry too much about and was now going to have to learn how to tuck away again, out of sight, if perhaps not as out of mind as she might wish—over the *ease* of it. Of simply being in the same rooms Caius inhabited.

After all these weeks they could predict each other's movements, in the kitchen as well as in bed. And there was something poignant and marvelous about the dance of that kind of intimacy. They hadn't experienced that before. There had been too much camping, too much hiking, so that everything was always new. Including them.

Mila had not expected the romance of familiarity. Handing him the utensil he needed before he asked for it. The way he moved around her, with the brush of his hand against her hip to let her know where he was, or the touch of his arm to hers because they were close.

The truth she did not know how to process was that she didn't know how she was going to do without this.

This forbidden intimacy she hadn't known she hungered for so deeply.

And this time she couldn't tell herself that the memories she had of him were overblown, that he was just a madness induced by those months of living a life she could never have.

Now he gazed at her as they sat before the fire. They had eaten, speaking in their new, slightly *careful* manner about things like history, change, and the march of progress, even in monarchies like hers. When she had suggested something sweet to finish off the meal, they had decided the best dessert around was each other.

He had risen, eventually, to bring the wine over and now they were sprawled out on the plush, cozy rug that was tossed out before the fire. She rather felt that they were in some kind of a cave tonight. As if they could as easily be ancient people doing ancient things, with only the light of the fire as witness.

More lives she could only daydream about, she knew.

"Are you throwing me out already?" he asked, mildly enough, but she didn't much like that, either. It was the way he sounded now, no longer all that marvelously textured gold. There was something like flint in it.

His wizard's eyes still gleamed, he was *right here*, but she couldn't reach him.

Mila hated it.

And she was making herself sick with all her *decorum*. With how much it cost to maintain her composure when they talked, if not when he was inside her.

It made her *ache*.

But, "I'm not throwing you out at all," she told him, and took more pride than necessary in how calm she sounded despite that ache, that sickness. How serene, with a glass of courage in her hand. "Yet in two days' time, like it or not, I will have to return to the palace. In all of my state. There will be no nudity near the fireplace, because what if the servants saw me? There will certainly be no *unmarried cavorting* of any kind." *Ever again*, she thought, and she meant to laugh. But the sound that came out didn't quite qualify as laughter, and that ache in her hardened into something far more precarious. "It doesn't seem like there's a whole lot to recommend it, if I'm honest."

"But you must do your duty."

Mila didn't much care for the way he said that, with that unmistakable edge to it.

Or maybe she didn't like it because it was true. "I must," she agreed.

And when he reached over and tugged her close, so she could sprawl across his body and he could set his mouth at her collarbone, she was grateful.

Because this fire, she understood.

Maybe it was better to stop talking altogether. That the way they devoured each other, rested as briefly as possible, and then went back for more was the only conversation that was necessary.

The next day they stayed too long in bed together in the morning. He rolled her beneath him, stretched out over her, and broke her into very small, very jagged pieces by taking it slow.

So slow there was nothing to do but *stay there*. In that gaze of his, all that lost magic she couldn't bear to lose again. In his arms, where she fit so beautifully. In the sheer, glowing wonder of this thing she couldn't have.

Caius set a pace that made her want to cry, it was so devastating. It was so shattering, so demanding, so intensely *revealing*.

He wrung every bit of emotion from her, brought her close to relief and then kept going, and Mila thought it was possible she would never recover.

That she would never feel clothed again, having let him strip her so naked.

She couldn't tell if she wanted to rejoice in that, or collapse somewhere and sob.

In the shower, before he joined her, she could pretend it wasn't tears on her face. She could prop herself against the wall and ask herself if it was possible for her to die from all this vulnerability.

Or if its curse was she would only feel as if she might.

As if she had.

She was the one who suggested a long walk to get the blood pumping more productively.

"You and I have very different definitions of the word *productive*," Caius told her darkly as they set out.

But she let the mountain do the talking for her. They hiked up one of the trails that led straight away from the back of the house, winding in and out of the woods and then out at last to what Mila believed was the most beautiful view of the kingdom in existence.

It never failed to soothe her. Even now, she could feel it sink into her, the sight of the lakes far below. The green hills. The villages dotted in the far reaches of the valley and then, far off where she couldn't quite see it, the palace she knew waited on the other side.

"It looks so beautiful from up here." They stopped at the bench one of her ancestors had installed a long time ago, because she wasn't the only one who loved this view. "It's beautiful down there, too, but from up here it's like a sparkling little jewel of a country, isn't it?"

Beside her, Caius said nothing.

And she was…less soothed. A bit raw, in fact.

That vulnerability did not seem to be going away.

Instead, it seemed to wind its way deeper and deeper inside of her, like a grief all its own. It made her wish that she was someone else. Anyone else.

It made her wonder, for the first time in all her life, why she was so certain she couldn't be—

But it was nearly October. This high up they were well into the fall already, and gearing up for the long winter ahead. There was a hard, crunchy frost on the ground, and it had already snowed while they'd been here. This high up, the air was bright and crisp, no matter how cold. The mountains ringing the valley were capped and white and more than ready for the colder weather that wasn't hiding its approach any longer.

Yet all she could think about was the man beside her, whose eyes glowed with more and more secrets by the day.

While she felt splayed wide open.

And it was something much deeper than an *ache*.

She thought back to that first night in the house. When she had let him in through the tunnels and he taken her right there on that couch. How when he'd stood up to get rid of his clothes he'd tugged something over his neck, then tucked it away before she could see what it was.

That was what she'd told herself anyway. That she hadn't seen it.

And she couldn't tell, out here in this confronting cold, if it was true that she hadn't laid eyes on it at all and had merely filled in the blanks in her own imagination, or if she really had glimpsed it.

She wasn't sure which one should worry her more, since both seemed tender. Both hurt her, if in different ways.

"You normally wear a chain around your neck, don't you?" she asked.

He let out a sound then. Too low, too ripe with the very shadows she was pretending she didn't see. "Be careful where you tread, Mila. You might find something you can't ignore. And then what will you do?"

She could already feel the different parts of herself fighting for supremacy inside her. It was easy to be *the*

Queen in the palace. Just as it was easy to be *just Mila* here. But this close to leaving the September House, both of them were inside her, pushing and pulling.

It was the Queen who sat straighter, lifting her chin. But it was the Mila who had been here this whole month who gazed at him, sure that all that vulnerability was splashed across her face.

"If it was a chain," she said quietly, so very quietly she almost wondered if the wind might steal her words away, "I think I know what normally hangs on it."

He stood up then, thrusting his hands deep into the pockets of the coat he wore. Like everything else that was his, it had been made by the finest craftsman and tailored to make him look even more effortlessly heroic than he normally did. Maybe it was simply that he stood at the edge of a cliff, his eyes out on the beautiful valley so far below while the cold wind moved through his hair. Maybe it was the distance she could see in his gaze, even though she didn't feel that distance between them, not entirely. Not when her body was still warm from his.

Not yet, something in her warned. *But you will.*

"How do you think I should answer that, Mila?" he asked in a growl, when the misery inside of her seemed to be at a boiling point. "Should I wrap it up into some kind of charming anecdote that we could tell at a boring dinner party? Is that really how you think this should go?"

She felt a kind of panic, then. It was the only way she could describe the sensation that washed over her.

It was the only explanation for the way she opened her mouth to speak, but then couldn't find the words.

As if her own hand was clenched tight on her own throat.

He turned back to her then and his eyes were glittering, as bright as the jewel of her country behind him. Brighter, somehow. Because her kingdom was something Mila gazed upon. But Caius's eyes tore into her.

Because he was the only person alive who saw every part of her. Who knew every bit of her.

And she was going to have to give him up.

Again.

"It's my wedding ring," he said in that uncompromising way of his, so at odds with the Caius he showed everyone else in public. But she had no doubt that this was the real him. She knew this version of him. This was the Caius she knew in bed. "But I suspect you know that. I wear it next to my heart. Isn't that a laugh? While I have seen no evidence to suggest that you possess a heart, I still think it might matter if I keep the ring you gave me warm with mine."

She was surprised she didn't topple over, that blow hit her so hard. "That isn't fair."

"I didn't realize that fairness was a part of this." He shook his head. "I rather thought this was an extended torture session. I will admit that I had aspirations for more in the beginning, but that will never happen, will it? You decided who we were to each other long ago. And heaven forfend the great Queen of Las Sosegadas change her mind once it's been made up."

Mila found herself on her feet, her whole body shaking as if she'd just run up the side of the high peak that towered above them. "That is quite a characterization. Insulting, but I assume that's the point. We've had this whole month, Caius. That's something I never thought would be possible. Why can't we take it for what it was?"

"I study the laws of your kingdom," he told her, that glittering thing still in his gaze. It made her shake even more. "It's become something of an obsession of mine. Did you know that the legal spouse of the heir apparent ascends right along with the crown prince or princess on the very day of ascension? A coronation is just icing on the cake."

When she only stared back at him wordlessly, the corner of his mouth twisted into that famous smirk of his. She hadn't seen it in weeks. She hadn't missed it.

"All this time I have already been your king," he said, and his voice was mocking now, with that bright fire in his gaze. Once again, she almost wished he would simply let her burn. "Some countries demote a man when he's married to the sovereign. But not here. This country has always understood who is in charge, as do I." He even sketched a sardonic bow. "Your Majesty."

Not *My Majesty*, she noted. As she was meant to.

And they both knew it was a demotion.

Her throat hurt as if someone really had choked her, but she made herself speak. "So we will end as we began, then? With more threats?"

"I don't want to threaten you," he threw back at her. "But I don't know what to do with the fact that I've been walking around with a wedding ring all these years. I don't know where to put that, Mila. At least before I came here I could pretend to myself that it mattered. That those months mattered, even if nothing came of them. That maybe you were out here living on that memory the same as I was, but you weren't. You won't."

He walked toward her then and for an exhilarating, much-too-telling moment, she thought he would sweep her up into his arms—

But he didn't.

Caius passed her instead and started for the trail back down to the house.

"I never forgot you," Mila said then, foolishly. Recklessly. And when she turned around, she could see that he'd gone still. He'd stopped right there where the trees were about to swallow him whole, though he didn't turn back. "And I still have the ring. I could never throw it away. I keep it on a chain myself and hide it away in a safe space, but I always know where it is." She wanted to stop there, but there was something inside of her that couldn't. That wouldn't. Maybe that was why she felt as if she was choking—maybe it was happening from the inside out. "I always know where you are, Caius."

She saw something go through him, like another gust of wind, though the branches of the trees around him did not move at all. And he looked back over his shoulder, his eyes brilliant there against the backdrop of evergreens.

"I would like to tell you that I would find it an insult if you thought you could call me up once a year to play house with you, *Your Majesty*." And her title was even sharper and more damaging this time. "But I think we both know that's not true. All you need to do is call and I'll come running. Like the little lapdog I suppose I've been to you all along."

He stared at her for another long moment, then he turned and disappeared down the trail. And Mila wanted to run after him, but her knees stopped working. They gave out completely.

She sank down heavily on that bench again, looking out at the kingdom. It was beautiful. Truly it was, but how had she never noticed how *distant* the kingdom seemed from here?

Because that was the point of all of this, she understood as she sat there, feeling far worse than simply *vulnerable* now. Thrones and crowns, rituals and schedules. The demands of aristocracy. The expectations of royalty.

All of it was to create that distance. And to keep that distance, day after day, year after year.

And this time when she cried, her tears turned her cheeks ice cold.

Her body followed, as if he'd never warmed her at all.

She couldn't stand it, so Mila got up and headed down that path herself, but she should have known before she got there that it was too late.

Because Caius was gone.

He'd taken her keys and left them in the door to the tunnels. She stood down there in the dim light, using the thick walls to prop herself up, for a long, long time.

It seemed to take a lifetime to climb back up that spiral stair. To wind around and around without him. To make her way through the cellars and back up into the kitchen that seemed to echo all around her without him.

Everything was too big, too empty. Nothing fit.

Mila decided that she couldn't face staying here for the last little bit of time she had left without him. The remaining time stretched out before her like a prison sentence. What would she do? Just float like a ghost through this house, missing him with every step?

The very idea felt like torture.

So instead, she called for her car and headed back to the palace early.

That meant she had extra time to turn herself back into *the Queen*.

She had to ride down from the September House and put her mask back on. Her armor. She had to root out every soft place, inside and out, and wall it up. She had to wrestle her body back under control, because the way she wanted him was *physical*, and still forbidden.

With every kilometer, she forced herself to remember who she was.

The closer they got to the palace, the more she reminded herself of what her life was, would be, and always had been. Who it was promised to. And what her duty required of her.

Mila is dead once more, she told herself as the car pulled in through the palace gates, and they shut tight behind her. *Long live the Queen.*

She woke up the next morning and surrendered herself to the team of aides who tended to her wardrobe, her skin care, her hair, and everything else concerning her appearance. She let them sigh and cluck over her as they repaired the damage of her month away, muttering over her cuticles and giving her hair what they called *a little gloss*.

Mila presented herself at a private dinner with her mother. Then she sat there while Alondra, seeming not to notice her daughter's mood, launched into her usual recitation of gossip, innuendo, and scathing commentary on everyone and everything Mila had just spent a month forgetting.

Back in her rooms, she could feel that ring in the back of its secret drawer, seeming to pulse like it had its own heart. Like it was beating to its own rhythm. Like it was shooting out light and heat, daring her to keep ignoring it.

But she did.

She got up and went out to her little viewing room instead. She wrapped herself in quilts. She got into her personal supply of wine, and she watched Caius's films.

In chronological order.

They were love stories.

But they were not happy. They were textured and complicated. They were tragic and they were beautiful, and she could see him and her stamped deep into all of them.

And so there, on her favorite couch, alone at last, she cried.

That terrible ache. That impossible grief.

Oh, how she cried.

The next day, she was absurdly grateful to throw

herself into her usual roster of meetings and appearances, and only slightly puffy and hungover after her aides were done with her. That night, she went to a dinner where she sat between two equally tedious self-styled *titans of industry*, where all she was required to do was nod sagely and make the odd opaque remark.

And it was fine, she told herself back in her rooms again that night. Once again refusing the siren call of her ring. The ring that *he* wore around his neck. Right there, next to his heart—

But it did her own heart no good to think of it.

It did her no good to think of him at all.

All thinking about him did was keep her up at night, watching the films he'd helped make. The films he'd tinkered with, like a mechanic after all, to create art while all *she* could do was sob.

And then suffer through her aides clucking all around her as they tried to repair the dark circles beneath her eyes the next day.

It did her no good to dream about him, either, because her body refused to understand that he no longer slept there next to her, that long, rangy body of his sprawled out beside hers, with a muscled arm tethering her in place.

A dream just like that woke her on her third night back in the palace.

He wasn't there, she knew that, but it took a while before she could do more than stare at her ceiling. Before the tears stopped sliding down her cheeks to make her ears wet.

And she couldn't fall back asleep.

But it was productive, Mila told herself, because she used the time to plan. Who she would call in her legal office to come talk to her about what had happened long ago in America. Who she would trust with that information, and who she thought would give her the best advice in return. Who, then, she could trust to hunt Caius down and handle him appropriately. So that, whatever else happened, they could legally be separated. As quietly and under the radar as possible.

Something she should have done five years ago.

Mila told herself that the emptiness she felt, that stunning desolation, was nothing more than a quiet certainty that she was on the right path at last.

And that was why she was particularly unprepared for the morning papers.

They were delivered without comment with the breakfast that she always took in her private sitting room. It took her a few more moments than usual to stop staring pointlessly out the window and to unfold the paper on top.

It took longer to stare at that picture on the front page.

Without a shred of comprehension.

Because she recognized the people in that image, but she couldn't let herself understand what she was seeing.

She was slow to put that puzzle together. Possibly because her brain rejected the possibility that she could be looking at such a thing at all.

It was a picture from the Garden Gala. She recognized the hedge towering there in the background. She stared at that hedge for a long while.

A very long while.

But she was quite certain that the only thing anyone else saw were the two people in the center of the photograph. Mila and Caius, doing absolutely nothing untoward.

That was what was almost funny about it. Of all the pictures that could have been taken, this was the most innocent.

They were simply walking side by side, coming out of the maze together.

But it was the *way* they were looking at each other.

She could see that immediately.

It was the way *she* was looking at *him*.

Mila had a look on her face that made three things abundantly clear:

One, that Queen Emilia of Las Sosegadas was a woman, made of flesh and blood and *desire*, not simply a monarch.

Two, that there was something unquestionably electric and charged and even *carnal* between her and Caius. The fact that the evidence was simply *right there* in the way they gazed at each other, even though they were fully clothed, somehow made it all the more blazingly obvious.

And three, the thing she'd been dreading since California had finally happened. The proverbial had hit the fan, with a vengeance.

She had finally caused the scandal she had vowed to her father she wouldn't. She had finally become the very thing she had worked so hard to avoid. She had betrayed herself in every way and worse, she had betrayed everyone else, too.

And now they would all know it.

While Mila knew that it was only the tip of the iceberg.

Caius Candriano, her one and only mistake, was going to take her down after all.

CHAPTER NINE

CAIUS FIRST HEARD the news that he was having a scandalous affair with his wife, a shock to all and sundry as neither all nor sundry had the slightest idea that Mila was his wife, at an arthouse film festival in Manhattan.

He had been working overtime. Not to promote the film he'd worked on that was being shown at the festival, because he felt the film spoke for itself. What needed his fierce concentration and total commitment was returning to his expected form.

Because Caius had never felt less charming or personable in his entire life.

One of his business partners had even commented on it the night before, looking at him askance as they'd circulated a private party in Gramercy Tavern, filled with all manner of gleaming, glittering people who were not Mila.

What happened to you? he had asked.

Nothing ever happens to me, Caius had replied, aware that his smirk was a tad more cutting than necessary for the sort of party that was all about creating connections and behaving like instant intimates, the better to extend their spheres of influence. *Ask anyone.*

In that case, let me talk to people tonight, his partner had said. *Why don't you just let them look at you. They like that.*

He couldn't even work himself into a temper about a comment like that. He'd brought it upon himself. He had lived down to the version of him that people wanted to see for so long that it was now all they saw.

And Caius knew perfectly well that the longer he inhabited that character, the harder it would become to tell the difference between the character and the man he really was, deep inside. He would forget it was possible. He would erase himself, one laconic bit of wit at a time, and this time, he wanted that.

The quicker he could disappear into everyone's favorite guest—the kind who never stayed too long in any one place, could be depended upon to provide the entertainment wherever he went, and never demanded anything of anyone—the better. He had let one person see that there was more to him and it didn't matter. She didn't care—

But he tried to stop himself when he thought things like that. There was no need to be unfair to Mila. Caius knew full well that she cared. The fact that she'd recognized the ring he wore around his neck and still had her ring too ate at him, with sharp little teeth and the occasional claw…but it hadn't mattered.

She could care about him enough to spend a month with him the way she had and it still didn't matter.

He needed to stop letting it matter, too.

He would. He was sure of it.

Any day now.

Caius had been prepared for the flashbulbs when he stepped out of the theater tonight. He was an old hand at paparazzi scrums and usually engaged them in conversation, got them all laughing, and generally did not behave the way some famous people did, as if this necessary evil that kept them a household name was a personal attack upon them.

As an old hand at fending off personal attacks, Caius knew the difference.

It was his habit to laugh off or ignore the suggestive things that paparazzi yelled at him, looking for that re-action shot. Sometimes he planted new stories while refuting the old, simply to entertain himself—because there was only one woman alive, as far as he knew, who did not want her name linked to his.

Tonight, that was the name they were yelling.

He shouldn't have stopped, but he couldn't credit what he was hearing. It took him a few moments of looking around to see if there was another Mila about to accept that this was really happening.

But how?

No one had seen him go in or out of those tunnels. He'd been scrupulously and excessively careful. *He* was not going to be the cause of any of her problems, whether he agreed that they were problems or not.

He did have some pride.

But only where she was concerned.

"How long have you been sleeping with the Queen?" screamed one fool who clearly did not value his life and would never know how close he came to a swift end, there on a street in New York City.

But Caius knew better than to react the way every-thing in him demanded he react. With prejudice. Be-cause he could not protect Mila without making this worse, whatever this was.

So he laughed, the way he always did. He smirked and posed for pictures with actors and directors and the people like him, who usually preferred to stay be-hind the scenes but could always smile for a camera.

Still, they kept at him with *The Queen, Queen Emilia, weren't you there all* summer and the like.

"Come on, Caius," a paparazzo he'd known for years complained as his car pulled up. "You need to tell us what's up between you and your queen."

"I would describe every woman I've ever laid eyes on as a queen," he replied smoothly, and with a grin. "You'll have to be more specific."

And he kept that grin on his face as the car pulled away, out of the pack of them, pounding on windows and shouting his name. He kept it there until it was clear that there were no paparazzi on motorcycles fol-lowing them, as sometimes happened.

Then, when he was certain no one was looking at him, he let his face…do what it liked. Whatever it liked. He didn't even look at his reflection in the win-dow to see what that was. Instead, there in the safety of his car on the way to a private airfield outside New York City, he pulled out his mobile and stared at it in frustration.

Because the sad truth was that he couldn't do the thing that every cell and atom in his body wanted him to do. Reality reasserted itself like a slap upside the head.

He could not simply *call* Mila.

There was no reaching the Queen of Las Sosegadas on a whim—that was why he'd gone to all of that trouble to find his way into her palace by other means.

The mobile phone she'd used in America had long since been disconnected and redistributed. He had checked. Years ago.

Though he checked again now, just to be sure, and hung up when he got the voicemail of a surly-sounding American man with an accent he couldn't quite place.

He had always known that he could reach her in person if he needed to. That was the story that he'd told himself for years, and he'd proven it in August. He could do it again now. It was easy enough to direct his plane to fly him back to Las Sosegadas. This time, he wouldn't need any kind of intermediary to bring him along. He was well enough known there now that he was certain he could show up, like an honored guest, with or without an invitation.

But what he couldn't do was call Mila himself and ask her if she was okay.

He knew she wasn't. There was no way they were coming after him and not her. She had to think her world was crumbling, and here he was, incapable of doing a single, solitary thing to help.

It was hard not to think that his mother had been right about him all along.

And that maybe he should have listened.

That wasn't even a round of self-pity. The person he was sorry for in this was Mila. He should have known that going anywhere near her would taint her with the same slime that he only got away with because he'd always acted as if he was in on the joke. The joke being him.

Now she had to pay for that joke, and he couldn't so much as text her that he was sorry for it.

The grief of that sat heavy on him for the rest of the drive, and it only got heavier. Once his plane was in the air, headed for his meetings in Hollywood instead of a tiny kingdom across the Atlantic where he was quite certain Mila did not wish to see him, he opened up his laptop and started looking for the story. Whatever it was.

It didn't take long to find.

There was one tabloid article after the next, videos from every outfit he'd ever heard of, and a great many he hadn't. Not to mention the user-generated content, which was far more scathing.

All of them using that single photograph to springboard into speculation.

He could remember walking out of the maze with her, but he'd been so certain they were discreet. It was something like an out-of-body experience to look at photographic evidence of the last five years of his life when for so long, the truth about the two of them had been something he'd thought only he even remembered. It was locked away, down deep, and had remained there until the summer. And even then, he hadn't really imagined that they would ever stand in the light. Not where anyone could see them.

But here was a picture that told every truth he never had.

Here it was, displayed in color for everyone to see.

He had to sit with that for some time. Because for all his brave words to Mila in the September House and up on that trail with the view of that valley she would always love best, the truth was that he'd never believed that she would ever truly acknowledge him. He had never believed that anyone would ever know that they had this kind of connection.

And it was hard to reconcile how resigned he'd become to that with...*this*.

He felt inside out.

With a sense of impending doom, he switched on his mobile.

A queen, Caius? came a message from his sister, almost at once. I should have known there was a reason you were suddenly so interested in that random kingdom.

Thank you, Lavinia, he messaged back. Your support at this time will not be forgotten.

It makes no sense unless there are ulterior motives, she wrote. But I know you always have more than enough of those!

Then she added a spate of emojis that he supposed were meant to indicate that this was a lighthearted response from her.

And this was his sister. The only member of his family he actually liked.

Caius sat back in his seat, staring out at the patchwork quilt of the American continent far below, wondering why his chest felt tight, his heart was pounding, and sitting still felt more and more oppressive by the moment.

Then he made it worse. He started looking at the comments.

And by the time his plane landed in California, he had saturated himself with more dire opinions about himself than anyone should. Or could, really, without going a bit mad.

He had meetings to attend, but when he got into his car, he didn't drive toward the studios. He drove for the ocean instead, feeling that same tightness in his chest. That same driving necd to *do something*.

When he got to the water, he turned right on the Pacific Coast Highway and headed north.

Except he didn't stop in Malibu, where he lived when he was in town. He kept right on going.

It was like something was chasing him, but he was pretty sure that the biggest threat to him was sitting right here in the car, inhabiting his body.

Everyone thought so.

Literally everyone. His so-called defenders, if such they could be called, thought he was attractive. That was it.

He had read hundreds upon hundreds of comments about himself and Mila on too many sites to count, and had not encountered anything he could construe as positive, save that.

Caius had expected to be called names. He could

even have guessed the names, without having to look. He'd made those kinds of names the basis of this character he'd been playing all this time.

Given that the Countess had often called him a great many of these names herself, they didn't really have the power to bother him anymore. He had cultivated his own image, after all. He wanted people to think of him as entirely insubstantial, so they could never be disappointed by him. And would never expect anything of him, either.

He was, as one scathing commenter had put it, *A man whore of epic proportions whose only talent seems to be showing up next to cameras where other, more talented people happen to be standing.*

That was all fair enough. But the more he read about people's disappointment in Mila for lowering herself to the likes of him, the less *fair enough* it felt.

Because it wasn't simply that they didn't like him looking at everyone's favorite queen. And they really, really didn't.

It was more than that. Her proximity to him in one photo made her a disappointment. It made the entire world question who Mila really was.

Caius could not think of a greater torture, and there was nothing he could *do* about it. There was nothing he could do at all.

The last time he had felt this powerless, he had been a child in his mother's neglectful care. He had vowed he would never let this happen again, and now it was not only happening in real time—it was happening to Mila, too.

His phone kept ringing and ringing, but he didn't answer. When he drove through Santa Barbara, he chucked it in a bin and bought himself a fresh new phone that no one could reach.

And then he drove. Low and fast, in a sleek little sports car that made him even more of the flaming cliché that he was. An embarrassment of such epic proportions that a single photograph of him with an otherwise beloved queen meant that there were calls for her to abdicate, so thoroughly had she stained the crown.

It wasn't his history splashed all over the papers that bothered him. He knew how much of it was made-up. It was the one they'd created for her.

As if he was so infectious—*A virulent strain of cringe*, one young girl said in a widely circulated video—that it was obvious she had to be some kind of liar and deceiver to have concealed this kind of thing.

He called only his assistant, to update her on his new mobile number and the fact he was not available, at all, to anyone.

Though he knew that if Mila really wanted to reach him, she could.

But she didn't.

Mile after mile, she didn't.

And that was why, in a tiny little town up north, he bought the supplies he needed, stashed his flashy car, and hiked his way back to the Pacific Coast Trail.

Because everything in him rejected the character he was reading about in the papers, because he knew that wasn't him.

But all he could think was that this was how Mila saw him.

This was the reason she'd walked away from him five years ago—and even now, after their month together, assumed without any question whatsoever that the only logical thing to do was separate again.

It hadn't even been a discussion.

And now he knew why.

He should have expected it.

The truth was that Caius had already been tired of the games he played. Reading about them was even worse. Cataloging the entire series of a lifetime of misdeeds made him feel sick.

It didn't even matter that more than half of the suppositions about him weren't true.

This was who people thought he was. Like his mother, they might have valued him for his proximity to fame, but they didn't value *him*.

He had turned into the Countess, he realized now. Entirely without meaning to, he had become a parody of himself. Just as she was.

And he knew that if he said this to Lavinia, she would encourage him to go talk to their mother because she still believed that there was some sort of conversation they could have that would fix their childhood. Caius knew better. He knew who his mother was. And better yet, he knew that the Countess would never see what she'd done to them. She would never admit that she had been in the wrong.

As far as he knew, she never had.

And showing her that they cared would be a weakness she would try to exploit.

There was no point talking to his father, either, because while the man might eke out an apology, all he really cared about were his highs. Caius had never been sure if his father remembered that he existed between visits.

All he was, to anyone and everyone, was that character he played.

Smirky, salacious, dismissible.

DISGUSTING! more than one commenter had typed. In all caps.

With every step, he thought about the fact that this was who Mila believed he was. This was the man she thought she'd married.

This grasping, empty, cardboard cutout of a creature, dead behind the eyes and good for absolutely nothing but the clout the entirety of the internet was certain he had not earned.

Hell, he agreed.

But for a short while, he had been a man that he was proud of. In a lifetime of make-believe, playing characters to manipulate people and situations to survive or to shine, there had been one stretch of time when he had only been himself.

That was what he hadn't forgiven her for leaving.

Their marriage was a symbol of that. The ring hanging there around his neck, still and always, reminded him with every step. It wasn't just that she had promised to love him forever. It was that when she had made that promise, she'd meant *him*.

The real him.

Those months had been extraordinary. No one had known who Caius was, and therefore, he'd had no influence whatsoever. There'd been no performance to put on. They had all simply…walked. And hiked. Camped and slept, then hiked on some more.

He and Mila had gotten to know each other as *people*.

Nothing more, nothing less. They had never spoken about their lives off the trail, not for a long while. Not until they'd left their guided hike and gone off on their own.

Caius had liked that version of himself.

Mila had fallen in love with him.

And this last month in her September House had been a reintroduction to that man. It had been a sharp reminder of why he'd long ago decided he hated what he'd become—the reason he'd gone on that long hike in the first place.

He hadn't wanted to return to that in the five years since, but he couldn't put the fact he had on Mila. That was what he'd done to survive the loss of her. He'd gone out and frolicked in that spotlight, acting like it had never happened and he was incapable of caring either way if it had, and this was what he'd won.

He'd made himself what he hated.

He'd become exactly what his mother said he was.

So Caius took himself back to the woods. Step by step, he walked away from the spotlight and the speculation and that goddamned smirk, and he vowed that he would walk until he found himself again.

Until he became that man that he admired once again.

That man that Mila had loved before she'd become *the Queen*. The man he knew she didn't believe he was now.

But he was. He wanted to be, for her, but mostly so he could find a way not to loathe the very sight of himself.

He vowed that he would walk until he found that man again, no matter how long it took.

And when he did, he would go back to Las Sosegadas and he would figure out how he could save the love of his life.

From himself.

For good.

CHAPTER TEN

THE PALACE WENT into crisis mode and stayed there. Teams of outward-facing staff huddled in the corridors, whispering to each other about *the situation*. The crisis management battalion took over all palace communications. There was a sudden influx of very serious people having very intense meetings, throwing around buzzwords and PR phrases.

Mila sailed about pretending she didn't notice. Or perhaps that it was all *beneath* her notice, which was not quite the same thing.

But when Carliz arrived, a few days after that picture hit the papers when it was clear that the scandal was not going away on its own, she was grateful.

More than grateful, even though her sister had left her baby, not quite a year old, at home.

"We don't get to see him enough," Mila chided her as she greeted her with a hug.

"This visit is not about him," Carliz replied in a fierce whisper, hugging her back.

Hard.

"How can you travel without your child?" Alondra asked that first night as they gathered for a private family dinner. "I know I never did. Not when you were both so small."

"You and Father did a round of extended state visits all over Europe the year I was born," Mila said mildly. "And again when Carliz was eighteen months." She smiled when her mother glared at her. "I've had to study the history of state visits, of course. What worked, what didn't, goals versus outcomes, the usual."

Carliz, on the other hand, smiled in that way she had that was precisely calculated to drive the Queen Mother mad. She had cultivated that smile, Mila knew. She had spent years working on it.

She had once told Mila, *If you can't be the heir, be annoying instead.*

"It is actually not necessary to live forever tethered to a child," she told Alondra languidly now. Deliberately giving the impression that she let her infant fend for himself on his Mediterranean island home when Mila knew she did no such thing. "As you apparently decided yourself in your day, Mother. I always knew we were secretly alike."

Alondra did not care for that comparison, as the way she gripped her utensils made clear. "I suppose that husband of yours can afford a fleet of excellent nannies," she murmured, quite as if her two daughters had not spent large swathes of their young lives in the care of staff.

"We do have some help," Carliz agreed. Serenely. "Though Valentino prefers to care for Centuri himself, whenever possible."

The Queen Mother blinked. "How singular that he is willing to babysit."

"He is not singular, he is a parent," Carliz replied, and she no longer sounded languid. Though she was still *sparkling* at her mother. "A *parent* cannot *babysit* their own child. By definition."

"You will argue about anything, Carliz," Alondra said, as if this conversation had already exhausted her. "My goodness."

"If you're asking if the man I married, the love of my life, is a good father? Yes, he is. And lo, just as he is perfectly capable of making empires out of all he surveys, he can also take care of *our baby*. Sometimes he does so when I am right there."

Alondra did not respond to that. Mila glanced at her sister. "I'm not sure she can take that on board."

"I'm sure you're both very droll," their mother replied. "I am certain there must be *someone* who would find your humor entertaining."

That person, she made clear with her tone, was not Alondra. She started talking of incidental things, deftly leading them all away from powder keg topics like anything involving Carliz's husband and Mila's *scandalous photo*.

So mostly she discussed the plans for the holiday decorations in the palace.

Later that night, when Carliz slipped into her bedchamber the way she had that summer she'd lived here—and every single night when they'd been girls—Mila felt herself relax for the first time since she'd walked down that trail behind the September House and found Caius gone.

Just…gone.

The crisis team had suggested he'd planted that photo, but she'd shut them down.

I am more likely to have planted that photo than Caius Candriano could ever be, she had said dismissively. *For one thing, he does not* plant *photos. He doesn't have to.*

But she had almost wished she could believe that he had. It would have felt like a message. It would have felt like *something*.

"So," Carliz said breezily, taking her place on the chaise. "It sounds like we have some catching up to do, no?"

Mila blew out a breath, and decided, what the hell, she wasn't going to brush out her hair. *Such a rebel*, she told herself sardonically. What she did instead was crawl into her pajamas and then curl up on the chaise with her sister.

Wine in hand.

She'd poured a glass for herself, and handed a glass to Carliz, who made an exaggerated face of shock.

"I see it's serious," she murmured.

Mila smiled. She took a gulp. And then she opened up her mouth and told the truth about her life.

She spared no detail. How magical it had felt to escape the palace all those years ago, and how she delighted in the so many ordinary things that her position had always kept her from experiencing. Being jostled on a street. Being spoken to sharply by a stranger. Being made to wait in a queue with everyone else.

Carliz was shaking her head. "I would not have thought that you would get off on people being rude to you, Mila."

"It wasn't the rudeness that was delightful." Mila shook her head ruefully. "I was being treated the same way as everyone else. Not like a precious heirloom that has to be carefully transported from place to place as if a loud noise might tarnish me forever. I liked it. It was novel and exciting."

"I personally prefer an upgrade," her sister drawled. "But to each her own."

Mila held her wine in her hands, frowned at it, and kept going. She told Carliz about her decision to do that long hike. The lure of going out into the woods and up into the mountains, away from everything that she was and would become. She told Carliz how hard it had been at first and how she'd second-guessed her choice—but hadn't wanted to prove that she deserved the cotton wool treatment by changing her mind. How she had made herself keep going, and had kept her complaints to herself, until the day she'd found she'd hit her stride.

"I didn't know that was an actual thing," her sister said.

Mila nodded. "From horse racing, apparently."

"Well," Carliz said over her wineglass, her eyes sparkling, "you have always been quite the thoroughbred, haven't you?"

And then, because it was time, Mila told her what it

had been like to meet Caius for the first time. How it had happened like the weather. One moment she had been contemplating her brand-new hiking boots and questioning her skills and desire to do this thing and the next he'd been there, drowning out the universe.

He had been like a shooting star. She had been dazzled.

And they hadn't exchanged a word for days.

"You must have known who he was," Carliz said, her eyes wide. "Everyone knows who he is."

"Of course I knew who he was. I only pretend to live under a rock."

Her sister laughed at that and waved her hand at the palace all around them. "At least it's a pretty rock. Let's brush past how you never told me any of this, shall we? Tell me everything."

And Mila felt guilty about the fact she'd hoarded all of this to herself, so she spared no detail. How they had gotten to know each other in a way that she knew she would never get to know someone else. Because the situation could never be repeated. She would never have that kind of time or space or anonymity. She would never be on her own again, not like that.

Back then she hadn't even been the Queen.

"He knows you in a way that no one else can," her sister said, with a certain wise look that told Mila things she wouldn't ask about her sister's marriage. "That's magic."

"There was something about being so far away from everything," Mila agreed. "I'm not sure that it could be replicated. Even if I wasn't who I am. Because he's who he is, too. And there was such an intensity to it—as if that kind of anonymity was sacred. Maybe it was simply that both of us were there for the same reasons. To be outside our skins. To find out who we were when no one knew who we were supposed to be."

Maybe her eyes got the slightest bit misty as she said that, too.

Carliz pressed her shoulder to Mila's. It felt like solidarity.

"You must hate me for not telling you," Mila said in a rush.

"Mila." Carliz shook her head with a certain gleam in her gaze. She reached past Mila and refilled her wineglass, then topped up Mila's, too. "Remember all those tabloid stories about Valentino and me?" When Mila only nodded, remembering that she'd thought back then that her sister would be the only not-quite-scandal of her reign, Carliz shrugged. "I planted them."

Mila gaped at her. But queens did not *gape*, so she snapped her mouth shut. "What? What do you mean?"

"It wasn't true," Carliz said. "We didn't have a re-lationship. We didn't *continue* our affair the night that he was supposed to marry, we started it that night. He would have ended that, too, but I got pregnant. That's the dirty truth. Do you hate me for not telling you?"

"As your sister, yes," Mila said, her head spinning, and not entirely from the wine. "As your queen? I'm delighted you didn't let me know that any of that was happening. My God."

"That's what happens when you fall in love," Carliz said in the same soft tone. "All of the noise, all of the trouble, it all disappears. And all that matters is the bright light that shines between you two."

"I did more than find it," Mila told her then, though her throat constricted as she spoke, so used was she to keeping this secret. "I married it."

And it took some while after that to settle back down. Because first there was the squealing. And enough shrieking that she had to assure the guards that all was well.

But Mila couldn't really blame her sister for this reaction.

It was actually...comforting. Validating, somehow. Because it meant that it was the big deal—the *huge deal*—that she had always thought it was.

She couldn't beat herself up for hiding this if her sister, who was usually impossible to rile up like this, was having this kind of reaction. Imagine what her mother would have done five years ago?

"I'm sorry." Carliz wiped at her eyes, still shaking her head. "You were far more composed when I told you my tiny little secret. But I can't believe you managed to hide something like this not just from me, but from the whole world. *For years*."

"I kept thinking it would come out. I kept thinking that I would wake up one day to find that he'd told the entire planet." She blew out a breath. "But he never did."

They both sat with that for a while.

"What are you going to do?" Carliz asked. "I know you were leaning in the direction of being the apparently not at all virgin queen for the rest of your life, but sooner or later…?"

She didn't have to finish that thought. They both knew what family they were in, and what each of their responsibilities were.

"There is no question about what I will have to do." Mila couldn't look at her sister anymore. She stared at the wineglass instead. Ferociously. "I must do my best to provide the kingdom with an heir. And, really, I was always meant to find the perfect king while I was at it. They have a list of the attributes this paragon should possess. He should be quiet and self-effacing. He should be weighted down by his own pedigree, someone who fades into the shadows while standing in plain sight, so as never to detract from my sovereign magnificence, blah blah blah."

Carliz reached over and hooked her hand over Mila's wrist. She squeezed until Mila found her gaze. It was too bright. Searing. "What's the point of being *the Queen* if it means a life of lonely misery? Isn't that just a nun? That's not your job description, Mila."

"Maybe," Mila agreed, astounded both that her voice was noticeably rough and that she did not feel compelled to hide it. "But what can I do?"

Carliz laughed at that. "Have you confused yourself for someone else?" When Mila only looked at her without comprehension, she sighed. "What if you just said, *Guess what? I love him. And I'm the Queen, so I'll love who I want.* What could they do?"

And it was easy, in a happy red wine flush and the joy of her sister's presence, to tell herself that was a good idea. That not only was it a good idea, but that it would be easy. A wave of the nearest scepter. A royal inclination of her queenly head.

But when she woke up in the morning her queenly head ached, her royal heart was sore, and she had to sit in on another endless meeting about *approaches* to the scandal. She had to nod sagely at the discussions of crisis management, sinking relatability scores, and *messaging*.

None of this was new. Only the intensity of these discussions were different.

And maybe she had changed—or it was the hangover that lingered at her temples—but it sat heavily on her that what they were talking about was her *life*. This roomful of people, mostly men in dark suits, was carrying on a rather heated *debate* about how she should proceed to live out what no one directly called her ruined life. Though it was heavily implied that it would all be picking up pieces and hoping for divine intervention from here.

All it took was one photograph that was in no way salacious to overshadow her otherwise entirely spotless reign, and the exemplary life of excellent behavior that had preceded it.

What she needed to do, she thought when the interminable meeting was over, was not listen to these crisis counselors. They were worried about a photograph and internet chatter. They didn't even know the real crisis, which was that she had given her heart away five years ago. Then frozen herself solid when her father died.

Only Caius had come back, and nothing in her was

frozen any longer, and she was finding it hard to remember why she had decided that the only way she could exist was to disappear into her role. Become a statue of *the Queen*, like the one that would no doubt stand somewhere in this palace one day, instead of a person.

She knew she needed to find that statue again, no matter what she could remember. It was past time to pull herself together. Get her armor back in place. Figure out how to wear *the Queen* like a mask again, but this time, never take it off again.

But first she enjoyed every moment of her sister's company. They saw old friends, like Paula. They spent as much time as they could alone together. Carliz had her speak to Valentino on the video calls she made and took to check in with him and the baby, so that at the end of the week or so she stayed, Mila felt as if she knew her brother-in-law in a way she would not have otherwise.

Better still, she had a sense of her sister's relationship with her husband, which, after all the studied formality in their family, felt like fresh air.

And on the last night of Carliz's visit, they once again indulged in a private family dinner. Because tradition always won out, no matter how many times the three of them had proved that sharing meals was a fraught exercise.

"I hope," Carliz said over the fish course, with a sparkle in her gaze that told Mila she was about to cause trouble, "that if we can agree on nothing else, we can agree on this. At least everyone can understand why even a saint like Mila would trade in her reputation for the likes of Caius Candriano. It doesn't need an explanation. Pictures of him exist."

"*Carliz.*" Alondra looked appalled. "Really."

Mila tried to look stern and queenly, but heard herself laughing instead. That did not make her mother any happier.

"The pair of you go too far." She pushed back from the table. "This can only embarrass the crown, no matter what the man looks like. *I* was never taken in. And I'm surprised that you, Mila, would allow yourself to stray so far from the path your father laid out for you."

"So you can call her Mila after all," Carliz murmured, eyeing Alondra. "But never affectionately. Only to chastise her. No wonder she had to keep a secret or two."

Mila should have stepped in then. She should have ended this with one of her usual serene asides that were actually commands…but she didn't.

"You don't understand, Carliz," their mother replied icily. "Thrones and crowns and the family legacy do not concern you. You've made that clear enough."

"By not marrying some terrible, boring man the palace selected for me?" Carliz laughed. "Guilty as charged."

Mila realized too late that this was a wound that needed cauterizing. "Mother, please sit down. It's Carliz's last night."

But there was no stopping her mother tonight. "You promised your father that you would never embarrass him, and what do you think this is? How do you think he would react to your involvement in such a tawdry scandal?"

"Returning to reality, it could be significantly more tawdry," Carliz pointed out. "All they were doing was looking at each other. Everything else is base speculation."

"If he was any kind of man, he would have immediately countered the situation. Instead, what is that clip that keeps running again and again?" The Queen Mother made an aggrieved noise. "Speaking of all his bedmates and calling them queens. It's disrespectful. It's beneath your station, Mila. I thought you understood that."

Mila stared down at her plate, biting her tongue. Something she was not sure she had ever literally done before, and it hurt. Maybe that was good. She was tired of her heart hurting, so might as well spread the wealth.

Carliz did not hold back, however. She fixed their mother with a direct, unflinching gaze. "Which sovereign's station are we concerned about here? Mila's? Or Father's? Because they're not the same person."

"Your father would never cause a scandal," Alondra belted out. "I can tell you that."

"I can't take this seriously." Mila didn't know she meant to speak.

Or maybe she did. Maybe something else inside of her was taking control at last. It wasn't that mask. It wasn't *the Queen*. But that was the trouble with all of this, wasn't it?

She was tired of *the Queen*.

She liked the woman she was when she was alone

with Caius. She always had. She hadn't thought that she could ever access that woman again—but it had been easy. All had taken was the way he looked at her.

All it had taken was seeing herself in his eyes.

Maybe she was having trouble remembering why it was she couldn't have that all the time. Why it was the end of the world to even want it.

She realized that her sister and her mother were gazing at her, waiting for her to explain herself.

That meant she had to try. She sighed. "I question why this is the greatest scandal of all time. It seems a bit unfair, if I'm honest. I have been a literal paragon of virtue my whole life. There are very few members of royal families who can say the same. And there's nothing untoward about that photo. We could have been discussing the weather."

"It's because you're such a paragon," Carliz said quietly. "People are so desperate for you to have a secret, dissipated life—one that makes them feel better about not living up to your standard of untouchable virtue— that they've created one out of a single photograph."

"People are horrified at what it means," Alondra argued. "That a woman whose passion has always been her duty to have her head turned by such a...wastrel of a man." She made a face as if she was disgusted at the very thought. Or as if it was Caius himself who revolted her, and something in Mila...chilled straight down to the bone. "It's beyond comprehension."

"You can comment on my behavior, Mother," Mila said quietly. And very, very coldly. "But I am not interested in your opinions on his."

"Hear, hear," Carliz muttered.

But Alondra waved a hand at her. "And now this. You are the Queen of Las Sosegadas, Mila. It is a little bit late to start acting out one of your sister's teen rebellions."

Carliz made a sound at that. But Mila found herself looking at her mother in a way she normally reserved for uppity ministers.

"Excuse me?" she asked, very quietly.

The Queen straight through.

But her mother's face was flushed with emotion. "I don't understand how you could let him do this to you," she cried. And when Mila started to speak, she didn't stop, which, from Alondra, was akin to flipping over the table. "Duty is everything. Duty is all that matters or ever will. It is the *only* thing you will be remembered for. Because we, your family members, will pass on and no one will know who you were behind closed doors. They will speculate. They will imagine as they please. But all they will *truly* know is whether or not their Queen did her duty. Duty is all that's left."

As she stood there, her face crumpled, just slightly. Just enough. But she caught herself before she could dissolve entirely.

Then, as her daughters watched, she pulled herself together in a manner Mila knew all too well. Because she did it herself. That deep breath. The straightening of the shoulders. And then, at the end, the determined rise of her chin.

"Love dies," her mother told her, in that rain-soaked voice she would never acknowledge. She had never cried in public. Mila and Carliz had assumed she'd cried in her bedchamber, but they had never seen it. If she asked about it now, Mila knew Alondra would say that was the tribute she was paying the late king. "All that remains is your legacy, and that only comes from your dedication to your duty."

Mila felt winded. She and her mother stared at each other across the table, and Alondra's chest might have been heaving as if she'd just run uphill, but her gaze was clear.

"And that is why, my favorite queen, only sister, and very best friend on this earth," Carliz said quietly, from where she was still lounging in her chair, "you must love while you can. As hard as you can. For as long as you can."

She shook her head when Alondra started to speak, and harder when Mila opened her mouth to do the same. "Yes, even you. Especially you."

Carliz looked at her mother, then at her sister, with compassion and something else in her gaze. Something like pity, Mila thought, though that stung more than she wanted to admit.

But then, Carliz was the only member of the family who had picked her own path. She had gone to university outside the kingdom, the first in the line to ever do such a thing. She had not toed the family line, married a palace-vetted candidate, and quietly produced children to bulk out the blood claim to the throne. She had declined the offer to take royal engagements, because she wanted the chance at a different life.

And Mila couldn't help noticing that she was the happiest person in this room.

Possibly in the whole of the palace.

"You have to make the duty worth doing by living a life worth claiming," Carliz told them both, with a kind of wisdom in her voice that made everything inside of Mila seem to ache. In rejection, she tried to tell herself. But she thought it was likely recognition. Her sister seemed to pin her with that gaze of hers. "Or what is the point of living at all?"

CHAPTER ELEVEN

CAIUS WALKED OFF the trail some two weeks later.

It turned out that he wasn't quite the callow younger man he'd been the first time, unable to imagine a life or a world that wasn't the same endless merry-go-round of notoriety and exposure. He hadn't needed months to come to his senses.

"Besides," he muttered to himself as he took the last long walk back into the nearest town. "The company this time was severely lacking."

With a couple of phone calls, he arranged everything he'd decided he needed, out there where his clarity had descended when he was finally alone in the wilderness. No comments section. No paparazzi. No one clamoring for his money or his notice or what he could do to *raise their profile*.

He could breathe again, and getting that back made it clear he'd lost it sometime over the past five years.

Maybe the moment Mila had walked away from him.

But out on the trail with only the sky and the earth, the weather and his heartbeat, he could think through the implications of everything. Every single thing that had happened to the pair of them since they'd met. He could see it all clearly. He could cut through not only the excuses he'd made to himself, but his own deeply ingrained, knee-jerk reaction to be only what was expected when people looked at him and nothing more.

How, the stars above had seemed to say, *can you ask for a change you are not willing to give?*

He had turned that over and over inside of him.

One day it had rained. On and on, relentlessly, and yet he hadn't quit. He hadn't even considered it. Caius had marched grimly on, determined to keep going until he found what he was looking for. That unidentifiable thing inside him that would indicate it was time to leave the wilderness and face the world.

Why, the mountains had seemed to whisper, *can you commit yourself so wholeheartedly to a hike no matter the adversity you face, when you accepted the end of your marriage without so much as a whimper?*

Caius had walked until he'd found the answers.

He'd walked into that last town, met his assistant, and drove the rest of the way to that same hotel that he and Mila had stayed in so long ago. Once there, he cleaned himself up. He restored himself to form, though part of him would miss the ease of the wilderness. The beard that grew without his notice.

The lack of any reflective surfaces.

He thought a lot about that, too.

And he decided that he could not let himself go so long again. That the moment he suspected the real him was retreating from his own gaze in the mirror, that was his call to take himself off until he found himself again. Until he remembered that he wasn't who they said he was. That was a role he played, and anytime he liked, he could step off that stage.

He'd had ample time to think through all those parts of his childhood that had led directly to where he was now. Caius knew full well each and every incident that had created the empty vessel he'd made himself into.

And he'd worked so hard on the particular quality of that emptiness, was the thing. He'd learned how to bend any room to his will from a master. His mother was a pro at it—it was only those who knew her who truly saw her for what she was. But her charm, used only on strangers, was a useful tool. It had helped him immensely in his business dealings, which was likely one of the reasons all the rest of his half siblings were in awe of him. Because they relied on his mother's fickle regard to fund their lives.

It had been good to walk until he remembered that he'd chosen the tools that he would take from her. That he had vowed when he was sixteen that he would never rely on her for anything material again. And he hadn't.

Caius had developed his pretty-as-a-picture, delightful, and profoundly empty persona instead.

He had used it well.

And now it was time to see if he could fashion a different role altogether.

Because he didn't need to return to this hotel room to remember all the things that Mila had said to him here on that last day. In their last hour. How she had laid out the gulf between them calmly, quietly, and had explained that the palace would never stand for it.

I am so young, she had said, though she had not seemed the least bit young then. Her gaze had been old and wise and sad. *They will question my judgment, and once they start down that road, there's little hope of coming back. I owe my father's legacy more than that.*

We all owe our parents' legacies something, he had thrown back at her, reeling from the shock of what was happening. The impossibility that he had found her, the own person in the whole world who looked at him and saw all him. And the agony that he could not keep her. *Most of us discuss these issues in therapy, Mila.*

Her face had changed then. It had grown sadder. Kinder.

Everything is a game to you, she had said, and it had devastated him. *That is what you know of the world, and you play these games well. But what I do can never be seen as a game, because that would make me nothing but a toy. And should that happen, how can I rule?*

Nothing that has happened between us is a game, he had gritted out.

But she had only gazed back at him in that same earnest, sorrowful way. *Caius. I am a pr—* Her voice had caught then, but she'd gone on anyway, with a certain resoluteness that he had thought might kill him. *I am a queen. It's time we stopped playing games of hide-and-seek, don't you think?*

"I do think," he said now, to the bathroom mirror.

He had not thought so then. There had been a part of him that insisted, always, that he had dispensed entirely with games and that she had treated him cruelly.

Now, all he could think of was the fact she had

waited for him to come out of the shower when she could easily have left without a word. She could have had one of her staff deliver the news. She had not had to stand there and talk it through, no matter how upset they both got.

He couldn't understand how he'd been too busy thinking of his own bruised heart, because she was walking away from him. When her father had just died. And she was going home not just to bury a man she'd loved and admired, but to take his place.

"You," he told his reflection, "did not deserve her kindness."

In fact, he had not forgiven her for it. Until now.

When he had set himself to rights, he crashed out on the hotel room bed, thinking that he would get a good night's sleep in an actual bed. Tomorrow was soon enough to set his various plans in motion. Tomorrow was the earliest he would even consider dipping a toe back into the life he'd walked away from again.

Another thing that sat heavy on him was how easy it was to do that. To simply walk away. This was the second time he'd done it so completely, but then, he'd been doing it all his life. Whenever something got too bothersome or too intense, the Countess had moved them on. He'd adopted the same habits, though he'd told himself it'd been for different reasons.

He couldn't settle. He was easily bored. He was always looking for the next great thing, and that meant a lot of moving...

At a certain point, a man had to face himself. He had

to stop running away and decide, at last, who he was going to be. The geographic cure was a lie.

He clicked on the television, flipping absently through the channels, though it was almost offensive to try to focus on flashing lights and gaudy colors after the serene stillness of the outdoors.

Though when he saw her face, on the screen and not only in his head, he stopped.

And then sat up, because it turned out that Queen Emilia had decided to make a speech.

He had plugged in his long-dead mobile when he'd entered the room, and he switched it on as the news desk of the channel he'd landed on talked about the possible reasons for the Queen to speak.

He found an avalanche of messages forwarded on by his assistant, but none from her.

Still, something in him felt called to attention as the screen changed.

And she was there.

Right there.

"It is not the habit of this palace to comment on the scandals of the day," Mila said in her calm, serene way, looking directly into the camera. She was sitting quite smartly in a chair in what was clearly the palace, that made her look as if she was seated on a throne without actually reverting to the Las Sosegadan throne itself. The light that fell upon her was splendid, but then again, so was she. Her dark hair gleamed, pulled back into an intricately braided bun at the nape of her neck. She was dressed, as ever, to perfection. He wondered if he was the only man alive who could see the passion that glittered in her gray gaze. He wondered if she knew that he could still see *her*. "But I find that I cannot remain quiet."

Halfway across the planet, Caius sat up straighter.

"I have been made aware of the photograph that so many have taken such liberties in dissecting," said *the Queen*, with more than a hint of frost to her tone. "I quite understand that there's an extreme level of interest in me and great speculation about my life, and I accept that. My personal wishes must always be held up against the best interests of the kingdom, and I can only hope that these things align. And that I always act with the country foremost in my thoughts."

She did not seem to move, but her gray eyes cooled considerably. "What I cannot countenance is the savaging of a man who did nothing to deserve these attacks but walk beside me at a garden party."

Everything in Caius went still. As quiet as if he was standing at the top of a mountain, with nothing but a sea of forever stretching out on all sides.

"This is a man who graces the covers of magazines with regularity, because he is a household name, almost entirely because of the genetic gifts that make him so pleasant to look upon. He can also boast a direct, hereditary link to almost every noble house in Europe," Mila was saying. "He is a favorite of style-setters and old guard watchdogs alike, because he is not merely pedigreed, he is kind. He is amusing, but never at the expense of others. By any standard, he would be a perfectly appropriate escort for any woman, including a queen. Indeed, the only reason he is held to be a disgrace, as I read to my surprise this morning, is because of the speculation in the gutter press about how he spends his personal time."

Caius felt almost...outside his own body. As if he was looking down from far, far away. As if perhaps he had actually died, hearing these words he had not understood until now that he had waited his whole life to hear.

The woman he loved, defending him. And not simply defending him, but painting a picture of him so that all the world would see him that way.

The way she did.

He found himself gripping his chest at that. *The way she did.* The way she must, or she would not have said those things.

To the world.

Mila did not seem to move, and yet the way she looked at the camera changed. It was as if she was demanding that anyone watching look within themselves and ask, *Is this fair? Is this right?*

And she wasn't finished. "I ask you, who are we as people if we believe every rumor we hear, hold it as fact, and judge each other harshly because of it? I am not certain who among us could stand tall in the face of such an onslaught. I am appalled that anyone should have to. I am deeply saddened that his association with me has apparently opened the floodgates to this sort of shocking behavior on such a widespread scale." She paused for a moment, then leaned slightly closer to the camera. "I have read a great many vile things about both him and myself in these past weeks. For myself,

I understand. I am a Queen. I am public property. But a man who smiles at me in a photograph is not."

She did not *say* anything like *You should all be ashamed of yourselves.*

But Caius was sure everyone heard it.

"Furthermore," she said, all stone and ice, "the world will know when and if the day comes that the Queen of Las Sosegadas requests romantic advice from the tabloids. Until then, I will walk in gardens as I please, with whom I please, and will expect my subjects to understand that I, too, have a life to lead. I hope to live it in a manner that will make them proud. But I cannot— I will not—live it to anyone's standards but my own."

For a long time after Mila's face disappeared, Caius couldn't move. He wasn't sure he breathed.

It was entirely possible, in fact, that he was really, truly having a cardiac event.

Or several.

When he ascertained that he was still alive, somehow, he swiped up his phone once more so he could watch that statement over again.

To make certain that he was not hallucinating. That Mila had said what he thought she had.

That she had defended him to her kingdom. To the world.

She had not spoken to him at all since he'd left the September House. She had not had her people chase him down to see if he had somehow released that photo, as he'd thought she would.

There had been no contact between them.

And that meant that Mila didn't know that he'd gone off into the wilderness, or come back a changed man.

"She doesn't know," he said out loud, in the quiet of his room.

She didn't know, and yet she had sat there and told the whole world not only that she would do what she pleased with him, but that he was an excellent choice. That he was a good man. That he was a worthy escort of an honest-to-God *queen*.

Caius felt as if something walloped him, hard.

As if he was a different man all over again because it walloped him so completely. He was surprised he wasn't tossed backward out of the room, across this haunted city, and into the Pacific Ocean.

When he stood at last—when he was *able* to stand— he felt drunk. And wild with it.

This time when he picked up his phone, he barked out more orders. Then he had to check the mirror more than once to see if he was in a proper state before he left the room.

Because he was fairly sure he was somehow wearing that statement on his face.

Caius wasn't sure he thought clearly again until he was in his plane, winging his way toward a tiny little jewel of a country tucked away in the mountains of Europe, and the only woman in his life who had ever defended him.

Not even his sister had done that. Not when her own neck was on the line.

In his family, it was always every man for himself.

The plane landed while it was still dark. Caius had

slept very little, preferring to rewatch that video of Mila again and again. This time, he didn't read reactions or comments—because he didn't care.

He cared about what she had said. He kept rewinding, looking for more nuance. Basking in her voice. Wishing that he could have reached through the screen to curve his hand over the elegant line of her neck. To feel the strength in her even as she spoke so softly, yet so resolutely.

Once in Las Sosegadas, he headed directly for the palace, prepared to charm his way in. One way or another.

Or cause a scene.

He wasn't picky.

Caius presented himself at the gates, expecting to be turned away. He was already formulating plans for that—

But it was unnecessary.

They made him wait, but after a while he was let in and ushered through the battlements, until he found himself in the palace's architectural wonder of the forecourt.

Where the woman waiting there, arms crossed, smiled when she saw him.

It took him only a moment.

"Noemí," he said, with genuine pleasure. "It's been a long time."

"Too long," the woman agreed. She still held herself like the guard she'd been pretending not to be when he'd known her. He'd instantly assessed her as someone with martial arts training and perhaps a military background, which was why he'd taken a closer look at Mila. And realized he knew exactly who *she* was.

Then hadn't looked away again.

"I never had a chance to thank you," he said now. "Those were magical days."

"They were," the other woman agreed. "And between you and me, I think we could all do with a little more magic, don't you think?"

Caius found himself grinning ear to ear. "I do," he said. "I really do."

Noemí grinned back, then nodded toward the path that wound around the palace and into the gardens.

"Her Majesty is enjoying an early-morning walk in her maze," she said. "I believe you know the way."

Caius started to walk, but something occurred to him. He stopped, looking back over his shoulder. "There were no paparazzi here at the Garden Gala. There were only official photographers." The older woman only gazed back at him. "And you are the Minister of Security, are you not?"

"I am."

"I would have thought that you would know of a photograph like that. That you would have seen to it that it did not slip out into the wrong hands."

Noemí smiled. She seemed to take her time with it. "Sometimes," she said after a moment, "magic needs a little help."

With every step he took, Caius couldn't help but feel the portent of it all. Back in the maze but this time, he knew where he was going. Back at the palace but this time, he wasn't pretending to himself that he was here for any reason at all save this one.

It was time to do what was right in the soul he'd always claimed he didn't have, and maybe he hadn't until five years ago. Nor since, as he was fairly certain he'd handed it over into her keeping.

But the good news about that was that he knew exactly where it was.

The maze was a blur of high, imposing hedges and his own impatience. Until, unerringly, he stepped out into the grove at the center the way he had once before.

Though it was changed now.

Summer had turned to fall. The flowering trees were bare. The pool looked cold and uninviting.

But Mila sat there anyway, as the first rays of the dawning sun peeked over the mountains and then tumbled down into the valley, lighting up the maze.

And bathing her in all of that shine.

"You defended me," Caius said.

He watched her go stiff. Then she whirled around and her jaw dropped open. Her gray eyes went wide.

"You're here," she whispered. "You're really here."

"How could I be anywhere else?" he asked. He searched her face, looking for clues. Answers. His own heart. "Why did you defend me, Mila? I thought I was your dirty secret."

And to his surprise, she turned all the way around, and then came to her feet. Or maybe he met her there in the middle. He would never know. It was all a brand-new sunrise and her gaze, wide and gray and fixed to his as if she was drowning and he was safety.

Caius had never managed to be safe for anyone, including himself. But for her, he would do it. He would figure it out.

"I hate myself for making you feel that way," she was saying, and there were no echoes of *the Queen* that he'd watched so many times on his race across the world. This was Mila. This was his Mila. "I hate that I wasn't strong enough to admit what you were to me years ago. I hate that it took all of this, all of this separation and all of these games I was so sure I wasn't playing, to understand what I needed, without question, a long time ago."

They drew closer together, in this secret place that felt like freedom to him. Because it was the first place he'd understood he hadn't lost her. That even if he had, he could find her again.

It was the first place he'd *hoped*.

"There has never been anyone for you but me," Mila told him. She blew out a breath. "And I don't care how many times you might have sampled those other queens you mentioned, because—"

"I'm a married man," he said, cutting her off. He caught her gaze and held it, because this was what mattered. This was a truth that had nothing to do with masks or charm or any of the smoke and mirrors he knew how to use so well. "I have never broken our vows. There were times I wished I could. But I couldn't. I didn't."

"Caius…"

And the way she said his name was like a song.

Something shifted inside him, then. All those blows

he'd taken since that photo was published. All the things that had become so clear to him out there on the trail.

There had only been one path in his life and it had always led here, to her.

"I'm happy enough to be your secret," he told her now. "I don't need you to claim me in front of the world. That you would think to defend my honor is a gift too sweet to bear."

"But bear it you must," she replied. "For it is a gift freely given. And I do not think it is the last of the gifts I will give you."

"I understand who you are," he told her, holding her gaze, because these were vows far more important than the ones they'd made five years ago a beach. These were the ones that counted, because he understood the two of them better now. "I always did. Of course you had to come back here and do your duty. I know that you always will. And when you have time to sneak away and make omelets in the kitchen with your own regal hands, I'm your man."

To his astonishment, her eyes welled up. Then actually spilled over, tracking tears down her face. "I think I will take you up on that," Mila whispered.

And he found himself smiling, wide and bright. And real. All of this was *real*.

No wonder the joy of it hurt.

She took a breath. "I don't know what you've been doing for the past few weeks—"

"I've been getting myself right," he said. And he

took a step closer. "To claim you, Mila. To claim my wife in whatever way she will have me."

And the way she smiled at him made his chest feel as if it was bursting wide open.

"I'm happy to hear that," she said. "Because I intend to claim you, too. And not as some secret affair who has to sneak in and out of tunnels to see me. I'm not doing that again." She leaned in, sliding her hands up his chest and around his neck. "Do you remember when you asked me to marry you?"

"Of course I do. We were muddy and sore and it's one of the best memories of my life."

She was still smiling up at him. "I always expected that I would marry one day, but it was never going to be like that. I was never going to get a surprise proposal, a man suddenly on his knee out of nowhere. It was never going to be based on love, emotion, sex. Any proposal that I could expect to receive would involve half the palace. A vetting committee. There would be many discussions and signatures. So you have already given me the most romantic gift that I could receive."

"I think you need more gifts, My Majesty," he murmured.

"I would like to return that gift."

Mila's damp eyes were fixed to his, and even though he could see the tears on her cheeks, he could also see that core of iron in her. Every inch the Queen.

But also *his*.

She didn't go down on one knee. She held his gaze steadily. "Caius Candriano, would you do me the honor of becoming my king?"

"I accept," he said at once.

"I wasn't finished," Mila told him reprovingly. "Will you be King Caius, my chosen consort? My liege man and protector as long as we may live? Will you help me do my duty, both in and out of the marital bed?"

"Your Majesty," he said, lifting one of her hands to his lips so he could kiss her knuckles, a courtly gesture from another age that seemed to fit this—and them— to perfection. "It would be my very great pleasure."

"And will you promise that you will always find me?" she asked softly. "Because I fear that it's possible that I might get lost again."

"I will always find you," he promised, without hesitation.

"And I will always love you," she told him in return. "Caius, I hope you know, I always have."

And then the Queen Las Sosegadas sank down onto her knees, tipped her head back so she could smile at him in the wicked way he loved most, and proved it.

CHAPTER TWELVE

QUEEN EMILIA OF LAS SOSEGADAS was perfect. Everyone agreed. And Caius surprised everyone—especially himself—by becoming an excellent King Consort.

If he said so himself.

But he was not required to say so himself, because everyone else said so, too.

Eventually.

There was an initial period of uncertainty, but he passed that test the way he had every other test in his life. And this time, he didn't do it by assuming that same old character. He did it as himself.

He stepped away from his life in Hollywood, because he didn't need it. Not when he had Mila. Besides, it turned out that he was far better at setting a scene and creating a publicity narrative than anyone on any of her crisis teams. He could do that job in his sleep. He did.

The best part was that all of the narratives they crafted were true.

In essence.

They divorced in secret so that they could remarry in style. It was the most lavish affair either one of them had ever taken part in, and they loved every moment of it. The bells rang for days. Holidays were called, viewing parties were gathered. There were celebrations in the streets, and his mother was not allowed in the country.

"I will accept nothing less," Caius told her.

"I will see to it you don't have to," she replied.

And as the years passed, that was exactly what they did. He piously applied himself to their most important duty and made certain that there was not only an heir, but a great passel of them.

And better yet, he gave his children gifts that he had never had. A sense of place. A sense of purpose.

Because Mila had set him free. And he, in turn, understood that he was her true home.

Together, they made certain the children would grow up balanced between the two. Aware of the duties attendant upon them as members of their family, but still free to make their own choices.

In his spare time, Caius worked on his passion project—a charity that created free cinema opportunities for children all over the world, to help them imagine something better than what they had. To help them wonder. To allow them a little joy when that might have been in short supply.

It took him much longer to win over his mother-in-law, but Caius was a very patient man.

"I always knew that you would adore me, Queen Alondra," he said as they danced at his eldest's wedding. "I've been waiting."

"You are a questionable man," the Queen Mother

said with a sniff. But then she smiled, because being a grandmother had mellowed her. Even she and Carliz had found a sweeter side to their relationship. "But you make a good king. Far more important, you're an excellent husband to my daughter. She needs both."

And much later that night, he crawled into bed with his queen, his wife, his love. He told her of his triumph, then pulled her close the way he did as often as possible, because there was nothing better than this.

The bright fire between them. The light that never went out.

The love that only grew with each passing day.

And at least once a season, they went to the September House, just the two of them, to make sure that they were still *them*. To get back to *them* if they'd drifted a little. To see the truth of who they were in each other's eyes.

Some years, that took a minute. Some years, there were conversations to be had, misunderstandings to clear up.

But sooner or later, they ended up on that same rug before that same fire, watching the flames dance and flicker.

And they found their way back to the real beat of their hearts that felt like one heart shared, one kiss at a time.

* * * * *